FIGHTING LOVE

MJ Mango

*To Megan
Thank you!*

MJ MANGO

Copyright © 2022 MJ Mango

All rights reserved

The characters and events portrayed in this book are fictitious. Any similarity to real persons, living or dead, is coincidental and not intended by the author.

No part of this book may be reproduced, or stored in a retrieval system, or transmitted in any form or by any means, electronic, mechanical, photocopying, recording, or otherwise, without express written permission of the publisher.

ISBN-13: 9798416152864

Cover design by: Art Painter
Library of Congress Control Number: 2018675309
Printed in the United States of America

To my husband...I wouldn't choose anyone else to live this life with. Thank you for your continuous support and talking me off of a ledge when I get overwhelmed. I love you always!!!

CHAPTER 1

Max's POV

It's a surreal feeling to prepare for what will be the best day of my life. In just three days I will get to marry the woman that I have been in love with since high school.

Audrey and I have been dating since our senior year in college but I have been in love with her since the day that I saw her walking into our high school. We didn't date in high school because at the time she was dating someone else but it didn't keep me from loving her.

When she finally gave me a chance in college I was overjoyed. And now three years later I am about to marry her in front of all of our family and friends. I don't think that I could ever be happier than this moment right now.

"Man, wipe that crazy smile off of your face." Justin said, teasing me. Justin is my best friend and he has been since we were about four years old. He knows how long I have waited for this day to come. He was there when I first saw Audrey and he will be standing with me when I meet her at the altar.

"How can I wipe it off of my face? Have you ever seen me this happy?" I asked.

"Man, I have never seen anyone this happy. I am happy for you. You have waited for this day for a long time."

I was surprised to hear him say that. I know that he doesn't care much for Audrey, he never has but he always respects her as my woman and I appreciate him for it. He is my best friend and she is my love. I refuse to lose either one of them so I am happy to have his support.

If it was up to me I would have married Audrey the day that she decided to give me a chance but I understood that her love for me needed to catch up with my love for her and now it finally has.

It's a great thing though that this is happening now. I am now established. I have my own company and have made a very strong name for myself in the business world. I am just a deal or two away from being a billionaire.

So marrying her now is great because I want to start a family right away and I will have no worries on how I will provide for them. I can provide their every want and need.

"Three more days, that's it. That's all the time that it's going to take for my dreams to come true."

I said to Justin.

"That's it. And tomorrow is the day that you and Audrey have to meet with your attorney to finalize things so be on time. This has to be done on time in order for things to be done on time for the wedding." Jason reminded me again.

"Of course I am going to be on time. I would never be late for this because I want it done and behind us." To be honest I hate to even have this meeting. Justin and my lawyer insisted on it though. No I am not getting a prenup or anything like that but my lawyer wanted to make sure that we came to an understanding about everything in our lives before we walked down the aisle.

If there is anything from our past that could create a scandal he wants to know about it. He has pushed for this meeting since the day that I proposed but I didn't want to offend Audrey. I personally have nothing to hide and I don't think she does either. It's just simply having things in order.

"Well, if we are done here I will head home for the day. If I am needed, let me know." Justin said as he was walking out of my office. Justin is my head of security or at least that is his title on paper.

He does anything that I need him to do whether it's to secure my buildings or hacking any system, he does it. When I took over the company I wanted him to be working right beside me but he insisted on being over keeping things in order. "It's my job to watch your back." he said and that's exactly what he does.

I guess I will head home for the day too. We are done with work and finalizing everything for the wedding so I am going to head home too so that I can see my love.

When I got home Audrey was in the kitchen fixing her some fruit but her back was turned to me. I could see that she had her earbuds in her ears so she didn't hear me when I walked into the room.

I walked up to her and snaked my arms around her slowly and she jumped. "Oh God. Maxi, you scared me." she said as she turned her head and saw me.

"Sorry, baby. I just missed you so much." I said before kissing her.

"I love you so much. I can't wait to marry you." I can't stop smiling at the thought of marrying her.

"Aww, Maxi." she said with a sweet smile.

"How was your day?" I asked.

"My day was great of course. How was yours?"

"It was good. Justin was riding my ass about how much I was smiling about the wedding." I said with a chuckle. She rolled her eyes, probably at the mention of Justin.

Those two really don't get along. Like I said

Justin respects her as my woman because of me and his relationship but my Audrey doesn't see it that way. She knows that he doesn't like her and so she lets it show how displeased she is with him.

"Well, everyone won't be happy for us. That's okay."

"No, he is happy. It was just light teasing. No big deal." Now I hate that I even brought it up. Maybe one day their relationship will be better because I refuse to choose.

"Well, enough of that. I'm going to get washed up for dinner. Ms.Ann has it smelling good in here." It was better to end that conversation so I left to go shower.

When I came back Audrey was already waiting for me in the dining room. We had dinner together as usual and then I took her to our room and made sweet love to her. Every time I am with her physically it's greater than the last. I can't wait to make love to her as my wife.

The next morning when I woke up I woke Audrey up too because we had the meeting that morning with the lawyer. I hopped into the shower and then got ready for the day. When I came back into the room I was surprised to see that Audrey hadn't gotten up yet.

"Audrey...Get up, my love. We have to get ready." I said to her as I gently rubbed her cheek.

Her eyes flickered open and she jumped up.

"Oh my gosh, Maxi. I can't believe that I fell back asleep. You go ahead to the office and you can just send the driver back for me. I will be ready when he gets back." she said as she got up and walked towards the bathroom.

"Okay, but he should be back to get you in about thirty minutes. Please be ready so that we won't be late for the meeting with the lawyers. See you in a bit. I love you." I said as I walked out of our bedroom and towards the front door to leave.

I headed into the office. On the way there I let the driver know to head back to get Audrey for the meeting. I got to the office and got my early morning activities out of the way so that they could be done before Audrey arrived.

My assistant brought me coffee and I checked my emails before heading to the conference room. When I entered the room my attorney and his assistant were already there and waiting for us.

"Josh and Tim. How is it going?"

"A lot better now that my favorite client has finally done what I asked of him," he said with a smirk.

"Yeah, well, it's not too late. The wedding is in three days so better late than never."

"Where is Audrey?"

"She should be here in a few minutes. My driver went back to get her after he dropped me off." Hopefully she was ready when he went back to get her. I hate to inconvenience people when it comes to their time.

For a moment we grew silent. After a few minutes I checked my watch and realized how late Audrey was. I tried calling her but I didn't get an answer so I was starting to get concerned.

Just when I was about to call my driver Justin came rushing into the room. "Gentleman, can I have the room for a moment?" he said firmly. I looked at them and nodded my head. They stood up and stepped out.

"Justin, what is this about?" I asked confusingly. He had a look on his face that I did not like. Justin is a strong and confident man but right now he looks nervous about something.

"Maybe you should sit down, Max."

"Justin, just tell me what's going on." I said firmly.

He looked at me and said, "Audrey is gone."

CHAPTER 2

Audrey's POV

All this man does is talk about is this stupid fucking wedding. I hate it. I don't love him. I never have and I never will. Being married isn't for me just like being with one man isn't either. It's not my fault that he was just too stupid to see it.

I tried not to let it get to this point but he just couldn't help it. I knew that he loved me in high school but who gives a shit. He wasn't my type. He was into books and shit like that and all I wanted to do was party and that was the same for me in college.

The year before we graduated college I decided to give him a chance only because I wanted the security that he brings me. I don't have to worry about a thing in my life because I know that Maximo will take care of it.

So, I agreed to date him and he was just so in love with me. I really did try to stall as much as I could but things kept getting deeper for him and so he proposed. I said yes but I never had any plans on marrying him. Hell, I'm not even faithful to him, not even a little bit.

I hate that he has ruined things for me because he is a heavy meal ticket. I could have pinched off loads of his money over time without him knowing it but no, he wants to fucking get married.

I was trying to find the perfect time to leave him before the wedding but it was never a good time. But when he told me about the meeting with his lawyer I knew that I needed to leave before then.

There is also no way in hell that I was going to let them into my past activities. Max may know of me but he has no idea about some of the things that I have done or the people that I have done them to or with.

So I planned all of this. I pretended to wake up late so that he would go ahead of me. As soon as he was out of the door I quickly changed, grabbed as much of my stuff as I could, and left. I did have a little sympathy for him so I left a quick note on the living room table for him to find when he realizes that I am missing. He will be fine and life goes on.

Justin's POV

My best friend is getting married and I am happy for his happiness and his happiness alone. I can't stand Audrey and I never could. It's just something that's off about her. I think that she is a liar and manipulator amongst other things.

She is selfish and doesn't love anyone but herself. Max is just so in love with her that he is blind to it. Max is a good person and he deserves way better than some half ass relationship that he is getting from her.

Ring Ring Ring

What the hell does Jensen want this early in the morning?

Me: Harris

Jensen: Sir, we have a problem. Where are you?

Me: I'm pulling up in front of the building. What type of problem?

Jensen: I will be there in two minutes. Wait out front.

He ended the call. What the fuck could that be about? Jensen wouldn't contact me unless there was a personal problem with Max so my nerves are on edge right now. I waited out front and true to his word he pulled up in two minutes.

"Jensen, what's going on?"

"Sir, I thought it would be better to give this to you." he said as he handed me a piece of paper.

-Maxi, I can not marry you because I do not love you. I never did.-

"Where the fuck did you get this?" I asked him.

"I went back to their place to pick her up. When I picked him up he said that she overslept so I needed to go back to get her but she didn't come out. I headed up to see if everything was okay and this is what I found. I searched the whole place. She isn't there."

"Fuck...Thank you, Jensen. Park out back because I will more than likely have to get him out of here soon." I said and he immediately got in the car to head around back.

Fuck. Fuck. Fuck. I hate that bitch. Who the fuck does something like this? They have been engaged for six fucking months. The bitch had six fucking months to leave and she picks two fucking days before their fucking wedding. Two.

I take a deep breath to try and calm down because Max doesn't need me to blow up right now. I have got to be there for him because I am sure that this is going to destroy him.

I head into the building and up to the conference room where Max is meeting with his lawyer. I fucking hate this. I walked into the room and had to take a few breaths before I started speaking.

"Gentleman, can I have the room for a moment?" I said firmly as I looked at the two of them. Max looked at them and nodded his head. They stood up and stepped out.

"Justin, what is this about?" He asked confusingly. I was looking concerned because I know that this is going to hurt him and I hate it. I am sure that he could read my facial expression therefore he knew that something was wrong.

"Maybe you should sit down, Max." This is going to be so hard for him.

"Justin, just tell me what's going on." he said firmly.

I took a deep breath and said, "Audrey is gone."

He looked confused. "Justin, what do you mean by she is gone?" he asked with his eyebrows furrowed. I opened the paper and showed it to him. Watching his facial expressions was hard. He looked confused and hurt.

I watched him stare at that paper for a few minutes. He slowly started backing up until he hit the wall and then he fell to the floor, still staring at that paper.

"Is...Is this a trick, a joke?"

"No, Max. I would never trick you about something like this." I understand why he asked so I won't get offended and anyway he is just heartbroken so he isn't thinking clearly. If he was thinking clearly he would know better than to think that I would do something to hurt him.

"Why? Why would she do this to me, Justin?"

"I don't know, Max. I'm sorry. Do you want me to find her?"

"Umm...I don't know." He said, looking dazed.

He didn't move. He just kept staring at that fucking piece of paper so I took it. "What are you doing, Justin?" he asked slowly.

"You don't need to keep looking at that...Come on...I'm getting you out of here and then I will make arrangements before coming over to your place." I told him as I bent down and helped him up.

I walked with him to the elevator and out back where I had Jensen park. Max seemed weak and out of it. This is all so fucked up.

I put him in the car before asking Jensen to speak to me outside. "Jensen, take him straight home. Don't go anywhere else and stay with him. I don't give a damn what he says, you do not take him anywhere else or leave him until I get there. Hell, I don't even want him in the bathroom alone. I understand that he is your boss but if you don't do as I ask, being fired will be the least of your worries."

"Yes, Sir, Mr.Harris." he said before getting back into the car.

I headed back up so that I could speak to his assistant and his lawyer. "Josh, can I speak with you for a moment in my office?" I asked as I walked up. He followed me to the office and I closed the door behind him.

"There will be no meeting today." I said as I handed him the letter. He instantly got angry. Lawyer or not he has known Max for several years so it's not just professional with him.

"Excuse my language but how in the fuck can anyone do something like this?" he asked.

"I don't know but this is going to destroy him. I will do my best to get him back to himself as soon as possible and you just keep any legal affairs in order. I will cancel all meetings for now."

"Alright. Let me know how things are going and I will do the same."

Next I spoke to Max's assistant and had her cancel all of his meetings for at least the next two weeks. I have no idea how long it's going to take Max to get back to himself but I just wanted to make sure that he had some time to process this.

Oh, fuck. The actual wedding has to be canceled. And him and his mother did most of the coordinating with the wedding planner. Shit, I don't want to have to tell Mama Mary this shit. She is going to flip. I think about calling my own mama so that she can tell her but I think that may make things worse because she is no better. So I reluctantly call Mama Mary and she picks up quickly.

Mama Mary: Justin, what's wrong?

Me: How did you know that something is wrong?

Mama Mary: Because I only hear from you when there is a need for food or when there is a problem. Since it's the middle of the work day I assume that it's a problem. Is Max okay?

Me: Umm...Not really...Umm...Audrey left him.

CHAPTER 3

Max's POV

I can not believe what I just read. How could she do this to me? This fucking hurts. This hurts really bad. I have never known pain like this. I love her so much. I don't understand how she can do this and to say that she has never loved me. How could she?

"Sir, we are here." Jensen said to me. I couldn't respond at all because I was lost. I just continued to sit there until Jensen opened the door and helped me out of the car.

"I'm fine, Jensen. You don't have to stay."

"Sir, Mr. Harris insisted that I do. I apologize but I have to."

I nodded my head and then he helped me up to my place. I went straight to my bed. I am still so shocked and confused. How could this happen? Where did I go wrong?

I don't know how long I sat there doing

nothing except thinking about Audrey but as long as I did Jensen sat right there with me.

I just didn't know what to do. I wanted to call her and talk to her but I stopped myself every time because she was very clear when she said that she didn't love me and that she can't marry me. That means that our whole relationship was a lie.

When I proposed to her why did she say yes? Why not just tell me the truth then? Why wait until two days before our wedding to tell me like this? So many questions are running through my head right now.

"Max, how are you feeling?" I heard Justin ask me as he came into my room. I just shrugged my shoulders because how does he think I feel? I feel like shit.

"I just wanted to warn you that your mom will be here at any moment. I know that it's not the time but I had to call her to take care of the stuff for the wedding." he said and I just nodded my head. I guess she was going to have to find out sooner or later especially since the actual wedding is only two days away.

A little while later my mother came in being very loud and extra. "Oh my baby. If I could find that tramp I would just kick her ass. How are you feeling, baby?"

"Honestly, I would really like to be alone right

now." I'm already tired of everyone.

"I'm not leaving you alone." Justin said with his eyebrows furrowed.

"Justin, I need to be alone to process this whole thing. I'm asking you nicely." I said hoping that they would understand.

"Okay, sweetheart. But promise me you will eat something and take care of yourself."

"I will leave the room, but I'm not leaving the house and it's not up for debate." Justin said firmly. As much as I wanted him to leave, I knew that he wasn't going to so I will take what I can get.

"Fine." I said and then they both left the room.

Justin's POV

When me and Mama Mary left the room she wanted to know every single detail about what happened this morning. I explained to her what I could but honestly I have no idea what the fuck Audrey was thinking. All I know is the bitch is lowdown as shit for this.

"Justin, promise me that you will take care of my baby. I want you to call me if he needs me, okay." Mama Mary said.

"Yes, ma'am." I said honestly because of course I am going to be here for him. I don't care what he says.

"Promise me or I will put Lindsey on you." she said with a smirk.

"I promise."

Lindsey is Max's little sister. He is only three years older than her. We have always had a flirting relationship but nothing more since I have literally known her for her entire life. Not to mention the fact that I don't think that he would appreciate his best friend dating his little sister. But more importantly, I was warned to stay away from her a long time ago.

When it comes to Max, Lindsey can be a bit much. They are very close and if she knew what happened she would probably be looking for Audrey right now. I hope that this situation doesn't get too out of hand.

Regardless of Max wanting to be alone I will not leave him in this house. I know how much Max loves that girl so I am worried about him right now.

Max has not come out of that room since he went in. He doesn't talk to anyone at all. I go in a couple of times a day to take him food. I also sit and talk to him even though he doesn't respond. I don't know what else to do to help a person that has gotten their heart broken by the only woman that they have ever loved just two days before their wedding.

But today, today I think it will be extremely hard. Today is supposed to be their wedding day. All I know is that I have got to do something to help…Now who the hell could be ringing the bell so early in the morning.

"Miss Ann, who is at the door?" I asked as I came around the corner.

"It's me, you handsome idiot."

Shit. "Lindsey, what are you doing here?" I asked, although I already knew the answer.

"Is that how you greet the love of your life, Mr.Harris?"

"Lindsey, cut it out." This girl.

"Okay. Jeez. Have a sense of humor for a change…Of course I came to check on my brother on this sorry excuse of a day." she groaned.

"No, Lindsey. He needs to get himself together and then he needs to talk this shit out and deal with his feelings. I can't have you going in there causing trouble."

"Mhm, whatever." she said as she walked away but I grabbed her wrist and pulled her back to me. I wrapped one arm around her and grabbed the back of her neck with my other hand, turning her face to me.

"Lin, promise me that you will not cause any

trouble."

"I-I.." she stuttered as she started to breathe hard.

I brought her face closer to mine and whispered, "Promise me, Lin."

"I promise that I won't cause trouble." she said slowly.

"Good girl." I said and then I kissed her on the cheek before letting her go.

She closed her eyes and took a deep breath before going in to see her brother. That fucking girl is going to be the death of me. I am pretty sure that she has given me gray hair already.

About fifteen minutes went by before Lindsey came out of the room looking pissed as hell. "Justin, I am killing that bitch." she said.

"Lindsey, calm down." I said in a panic.

"No. That's not even my sweet brother in there. It's like he is in a shell. He isn't talking. He is just sitting there looking cold and heartless. She left him and took his soul with her. If I see the bitch it's her ass and I mean it."

I knew at this point there was nothing that I could say to calm her down. If Lindsey ever sees Audrey she will definitely be losing her shit.

"Lindsey, just try to keep a cool head. Don't make trouble for Max which will in turn make trouble for me."

"Whatever, Justin. I'm leaving. Take care of my brother." she said as she headed out of the door.

I took a deep breath before heading to Max's room to check on him. Just as Lindsey said he was sitting there looking like a shell. His eyes looked cold and mean. He looked nothing like the happy and friendly person that he is.

I tried my best to talk to him and I tried to get him to express himself instead of keeping it in but I got nothing.

Another day went by with Max doing the exact same thing. I had decided that I would just go back to work on Monday to help run the office and get someone else to come sit at the house. However when Monday came around before I could even get ready he came walking out of the his bedroom door, shocking the fuck out of me.

He was dressed in all black with dark shades on. "Max, you're up." I said shockingly.

"Yes, I will see you at the office." He sounded dry and cold.

"But, Max, we need to talk." I said to him but he kept walking.

This is not good. I know Max. If he doesn't work his feelings out it will be a bad situation for everyone. Fuck. I guess I better hurry up before he terrorizes the whole damn office building.

CHAPTER 4

Max's POV

I can't take this shit anymore. I have done nothing but sit in my room for days. At one point I thought that I wouldn't make it. I felt like just laying there and giving up but thankfully Justin wouldn't let me. He stayed with me and made sure that I at least ate and got some rest.

I am thankful but now it's time to get up. I sulked for days and went through our wedding day feeling like I would die from heartbreak but I didn't so it's time to get up. It's time to move on and put my life back together. People get their hearts broken every day. Life goes on.

I get out of bed, shower, and get dressed. When I walked out of my room Justin was surprised to see me and he tried to stop me from leaving. He keeps trying to get me to talk about my feelings but that's not something that I am willing to do. Why would I willingly talk about the worst moment of my life?

I left him there still looking shocked and headed to the office. I have a business to run. I have no time to sit around talking about feelings and shit.

"Morning, Sir." My assistant said as I walked into the office. She looked surprised as hell to see me. I hated walking through the office while everyone gave me sympathetic looks and sad smiles. The shit is fucking embarrassing.

The first thing that I do is check my emails and once again get embarrassed because several business partners emailed me to give me sympathy for what Audrey had done. Most of them received an invitation to the wedding and had to be told about the cancellation otherwise they wouldn't know.

I started responding to emails about business only because I won't be discussing my personal life with anyone. Not long after Justin came in for our usual Monday morning meeting.

I can tell that he wanted to say something but he knows that I always take care of business before speaking to anyone on a personal level. Today will be no different. As soon as we were done he started with his shit.

"So, Max, talk to me, man. How are you feeling?" he asked me.

"Justin, I don't want to talk about my personal

life. Please leave it where it belongs."

"Man, you can't bottle that shit up. It will only hurt you more in the long run." He has been saying this same shit for days.

"Get back to work." I groaned before turning towards my computer to work. I'm not doing this shit with anyone and I fucking mean it.

I have to admit that it was a little rough to get through my day but I was doing it. About halfway through the workday I had caught up with all of my business emails and had a couple of meetings too.

Justin comes walking in with my tray all of a sudden. "What are you doing with my tray?" I asked him.

"Bringing you your lunch."

"And why are you bringing it instead of the person whose job it is?" I asked confusingly.

"Because of the way you have been so firm and grouchy today, everyone is nervous and scared to come in here. She asked me to bring it to you." he said, causing me to sigh in frustration.

"I really don't give a damn how grouchy I am, I pay her to do a job and that's what she will do."

"Max, you need to work out your heartbreak."

"Will you stop bringing that shit up? I am fine." I said to him, getting irritated.

"Max, have you ever heard the saying "if you don't heal from what hurt you, you will bleed on people who didn't cut you?" he asked.

I think about it for a moment. "No, I haven't."

"Well, think about that for a moment. No one here has done anything wrong to you. Now you may not want to get personal with anyone but everyone deserves respect until they show otherwise. Remember that." he said before getting up to leave my office.

The rest of my day went by without me having any issues. I thought about what Justin said and he was right. I will distance myself from them but I can be respectful and not be an asshole.

I stayed in the office that day pretty late. It had been days since I worked so I needed to catch up on some things. I also figured that I had nothing to go home to so I may as well just work. It was past ten when Justin came into my office to drag me out.

"I thought that you were gone." I said to him with my eyebrows furrowed.

"I was gone. Jensen called to let me know that he was still waiting for you. He needed to get home to his family. Let's go." he said firmly.

"Fuck. Give me a second." I said as I shut down my computer and packed up my bag. "Let Jensen know that I will drive myself home for at least the next couple of days because I will be working late." Once I was done I walked past him to go to the elevator.

We rode to my house in a silence that I welcomed. I am thankful for a friend like Justin but he needs to understand that I just can't talk about what happened. This is my way of dealing with it.

When I got home it was hard I admit. It was the first time in years that I had come home from work and she wasn't there waiting for me. I ate the food that Miss Ann had prepared for me before I headed to my room to shower.

I showered and just tried to relax under the water but my thoughts kept going to what she had done to me. I had to get out of there. I had to get out of that room. My room was nothing but a constant reminder of the memories that we shared. For that reason I decided to start sleeping in one of my guest rooms and have Miss Ann bring some of my stuff to the other end of the apartment.

This became my new normal for quite a while. I woke up, went to work, held meetings, and came home. There was nothing else for me. I didn't care to see anyone or to do anything. My only wish was to eventually get over the pain that I was feeling.

I knew that one day I would be okay because I believe that time would heal my wounds. Until then I would just live my life as best as I could.

I often wondered what Audrey was doing or how she felt after the break up. Not one time did I hear from her or anyone that she is friends with or her family. It was like we never knew each other.

As bad as I wanted to not give a damn I did. I cared a lot and I hated that shit. But then one day I just woke up and I felt okay. I felt like I could breathe freely again. Life was beginning to be normal for me again and I was thankful for it.

CHAPTER 5

Max's POV (several months later)

Life has been a whole lot better for me lately. I feel like my wounds are closing. I rarely think about Audrey now although when I do think about her the hurt is no less painful. I have since moved back into my bedroom and I am not working so late anymore.

Justin has also made it his mission to get my social life back in order. When all of this happened I stopped attending events because I didn't want anyone to ask me questions about Audrey. After a while Justin convinced me to go to a few and I have actually been having a really good time.

I am currently headed into the office for what will be one long ass day. I have two major deals to work on that will close tomorrow so I don't have time for any bullshit.

"Wait...Stop the car." I said to Jensen. I turned to study what I am seeing and fuck, it can't be. I stepped out of the car and approached the woman.

"A-Audrey?" I said. She looked like she froze at the sound of my voice.

"Audrey, what's going on? I don't understand. Are you p-pregnant?" I asked her. Of course she is fucking pregnant. I'm staring at her round belly but fuck, is it mine.

"Umm...Of course I am pregnant, Maxi."

"Is the baby mine?" I asked her. She tensed up, but didn't say anything. "Audrey? Please say something. Please." I begged her.

"Maxi, I never intended for you to find out." What the hell? What is wrong with her? I have never known someone to act so heartless to someone that has done nothing but care for them.

"Audrey, can we go somewhere to talk, please? It can be anywhere you choose." I said. She didn't say anything for a moment but then she finally nodded her head. "Thank you. The car is right over here."

"So, where are we talking?" I asked.

"Your place is fine."

"Jensen, take us back to my place."

When we got to my building I helped her out of the car before we walked in. The elevator ride seemed long as fuck. I am trying my best to reel in my emotions but I don't know how to feel right now. Audrey is pregnant with my baby and she wasn't even going to tell me. Regardless of what she has done I need to control how I am feeling because I don't want her to be stressed while she is pregnant.

"Have a seat." I motioned towards the couch while I took a seat on the other one that's across from her. I took a deep breath because I am really trying to stay calm right now.

"So, why didn't you contact me in any way to let me know about you being pregnant?" I asked her.

"As I said previously, I do not love you and I don't want to be with you." she said to me without a hint of any kind of emotion.

"Audrey, I understand that. Trust me, I got the message loud and clear but don't you think that I have the right to be in my child's life?"

"I just don't want things to be complicated. I would prefer for it to be just me and my baby."

"Audrey, I'm not asking you to be with me at all. But don't you think that what you are doing isn't fair to me? Is it fair to our baby?"

She seems to be thinking for a minute which confuses me because what the fuck is there to think about. How dare she want to keep my baby from me?

"I guess it's not." she finally says.

"And you're sure that this baby is mine?" I asked her and she had the nerve to look at me as if I insulted her.

"Audrey, I'm not trying to be rude, but I just want to confirm."

"Of course this is your baby. We were engaged, remember. Who else would I be sleeping with?" she said matter of factly.

"Okay, well I want to be there. I am by no means asking you to be with me or for us to be a family. I just want to be there for my kid. I need to be there. Please, Audrey." I begged her.

"Maxi, I don't know." she said. I got up and walked over to sit next to her.

"Audrey, please. I can't have a child out there somewhere and just not be a part of his or her life. I can't do that. Please. Let me be there for my baby and for the rest of the pregnancy. I promise you that I won't get in the way of what you want for yourself but I need my baby." I pleaded with her.

After staring at me for a few seconds she finally said yes. I had to keep myself from screaming with excitement. I didn't want to force her but there was no way that I wasn't going to be in my child's life. I just felt that it was better to get her to agree than to run to the courts.

"Thank you, Audrey...Do you mind if I rub your stomach?" I asked her.

"Sure, go ahead." she mumbled.

I started rubbing her stomach and the feeling was so surreal. I can't believe that I am going to be a dad. I can't wait to be able to hold my little one in my arms.

"So, do you know what we are having?" I asked.

"A girl." she said, causing me to smile even harder. I'm going to have a daughter, my baby girl. Fuck, I can't wait.

"When will she get here?"

"I have three more weeks until my due date, so not long at all."

"Wow. So we need to work out some details then. I want to make sure that you all have what you need and that you don't have any worries right now."

And that's exactly what we did. We sat down and talked about everything from the moment that she realized that she was pregnant to the plans that we have for when my baby girl gets here. The whole time I kept rubbing on her stomach. I have missed so much of her pregnancy and I just want to be here for it all.

We were talking about the baby and things were going great. I do not have a desire to be with Audrey but I feel the need to make sure that she is taken care of while she is pregnant with my child.

Everything was going great as I said until I heard the front door open and close.

Justin's POV

When I got to the office this morning I went into Max's office for our morning meeting as always. We always have this meeting to go over any new security measures as well as anything else that I need to handle for him. The problem this morning was that he was nowhere to be seen.

I waited for a few minutes but he still didn't show up so I asked his assistant where he was and was told that he didn't come in this morning. That isn't like him to not show up without letting me or someone else know so I gave him a call but I didn't get an answer. I decided to call Jensen since he is Max's personal driver.

Jensen: Morning, Mr.Harris.

Me: Jensen, where is Max? Did I miss something on his schedule?

Jensen: No, Sir, you didn't. He actually had to come back home.

Me: For what?

Jensen: I'm not sure that I should say, Sir, but I think that you may need to come here.

Me: Okay

I ended the call and immediately headed to Max's house. I wonder what the fuck could be going on because from the way that Jensen sounded it was if he was in shock a little. I started to think that maybe Max was having a bad day about the break up because he does sometimes.

I was not prepared for what I actually saw when I walked through the door. Not this bitch. Nope. Uh-uh. I am trying to calm the fuck down but I can't.

"What the fuck is she doing here?" I asked Max who looked shocked to see me.

"Justin…Umm…We can talk about that later. It's okay." he said. What the fuck?

"No it's not okay. So, what is she trying to do, pin her baby on you now?"

"No. I saw her. She wasn't even going to tell me. Calm down, Justin. I don't want her to get upset."

I just looked at him because I was so confused. Max is one book smart motherfucker but when it comes to common sense he just doesn't have a fucking clue.

"You tell Max what you have been up to these months while you were gone. You tell him where you went when you left him. Tell him about all of the men that you have been with." I said to her and she just sat there wide eyed.

"You checked up on her? I told you that I didn't want to know." he said as if he was offended.

"Yeah, you did. But did you really think that bitch was going to do you like that and I wasn't going to find out what the fuck was going on. Really?"

Max looked back at Audrey and she had tears in her eyes. I shook my head because I knew that it hurt him to see her crying if he thinks that she is having his baby.

"Justin, I'm going to have to see you at the office. I can't have you upsetting Audrey and causing her stress."

"I tell you what, I will leave. That's fine. But just as I have been here since we were four years old and when she left the first time, I will be here when she leaves again."

I said and I was going to leave it at that until she mumbled, "I'm not going anywhere."

I turned to face her. "Oh yes the hell you are. As soon as that blood test comes back negative, not only will you be leaving this fucking house but I'm letting Lindsey loose on your ass." I said before walking out of the fucking door.

CHAPTER 6

Max's POV

To be honest that was a little unexpected. First of all I wasn't expecting to even see Justin at my place but when I checked my phone I realized that he did try to call me first.

I know that Justin doesn't care for Audrey but I definitely wasn't expecting him to blow up on her like that. It kind of hurts to know that he doesn't trust me on this or that he doesn't care enough to not want to put my child's mother through that. It's shocking because that's not how he usually is.

After he left I had to take a moment to gather myself. I turned to Audrey and she still looked upset. "Audrey, I'm sorry that you had to go through that. I will make sure that he doesn't come by the house when you're here. I don't want you to be upset. Our baby is my main priority." I assured her.

I just didn't want to give her a reason to not want me around so I will just make sure that those two don't run into each other. I took a deep breath and just shook my head. This is going to be something else.

"Well, Audrey, I need to get to the office because I have some important things to take care of. I can have Jensen take you where you need to go or you can stay here and rest, but please don't disappear on me right now." I pleaded with her.

"I won't, Maxi. He can take me home and that way he will know where I live. I will also unblock you so that you can call me." I just looked at her and nodded my head. She blocked me. I thought that she had gotten another number.

We got in the car so that Jensen could take us where we needed to go. When I got to the office I looked at Audrey and said, "Thank you again for agreeing to let me be there. Please take care of my baby girl." She nodded her head before I stepped out of the car and went into my office.

I got started on my work and was trying to catch up from the things that I had to put off this morning. A little while later Justin came in for the meeting that we should have had this morning. Once we were done with the meeting he stood up to leave but I stopped him.

"Justin, can we talk for a moment?" I asked and he turned back around.

"Sure."

"I was a bit surprised at your reaction earlier."

"I don't know why. You know how I feel about her."

"Yeah, but can't you get along with her for me? Can't you just be there and support me on this?" I asked him.

"I'm sorry, Max, but I can't support you being with that bitch."

"Justin...Why would you keep calling her that?" I asked him.

"I don't usually call women out of their name but she isn't a woman. She is a liar and a manipulator." he groaned.

"Justin, you are my best friend and she is the mother of my child. Are you really going to make me choose between you and my baby?" I asked him with my eyebrows furrowed.

"Of course I wouldn't do that, Max."

"Then, please. I need your support on this. Not for Audrey but for me." His face softened a little before he spoke.

"Okay, Max. I will support *you* on this, only you." I guess that is better than nothing.

"Thank you, man." I said and he just hummed before leaving my office.

The next few weeks were actually amazing.

Me and Audrey had been communicating regularly and I was able to make a couple of her doctor's appointments. It was such an amazing feeling to see my baby girl on the monitor and to hear her heartbeat.

We had gone out and bought everything that we would need for the baby for both her place and mine. We also decided that for the first few weeks or so that she would stay at my place in the guest room that is next to my nursery.

I was happy with that. I wasn't going to lose a precious moment with the baby and neither would she. Now we are just playing the waiting game. She has been having mild contractions but nothing major.

I reluctantly made the decision to get a dna test at birth like Justin suggested. Audrey said that she wasn't sleeping with anyone else but I think that it would be best to get it over with. I don't want my family or anyone else to not be accepting of my baby because they have doubts so I want to confirm.

I did tell my family about Audrey being pregnant. My dad stayed silent which I am not surprised about at all. If he doesn't have anything nice to say he isn't going to say it. My mom, although doubtful, said that she would support me. Lindsey is a completely different story. She was livid and had the worst reaction out of everyone including Justin.

As a matter of fact I haven't spoken to her or seen her in a couple of weeks. She said that it would be best if she stayed away until the baby was born. I agreed with her. Lindsey could lose her shit and snap. I can't have that.

Knock Knock

"Come in." I said. It was my assistant. "Yes, Darla. What do you need?"

"Sir, when do you want me to schedule your meeting? I know that you were keeping your schedule open for when Audrey goes into labor."

"Umm...Let me get back to you on that. It will probably have to wait a couple of weeks."

"Okay. Will do." She said and just as she exited the room my phone rang. I looked down to see that it was Audrey calling.

Me: Hey.

Audrey: Hey, Maxi. I think that it's time. My contractions are getting closer.

Me: Okay. I am on the way. Are you at home?

Audrey: Yes.

Me: Okay. I'm coming.

I hung up and rushed out of the door. Jensen was parked right out front as always. "Jensen, take me to Audrey's. She is in labor so step on it." I said with excitement. I shot Justin a text to let him know why I was out of the office so that he can make sure that everything is in order.

We soon arrived at Audrey's place. I got out so that I could help her into the car. Thankfully she was waiting downstairs because as soon as we walked out of the door her water broke. Fuck. We have to hurry up now.

"Maxi.." she said with a look of panic.

"It's going to be okay, Audrey. I'm right here with you." I said, trying to comfort her.

I helped her in and we headed to the hospital. As soon as we arrived they sent her up to a room and started hooking her up and getting her prepared. I am a little shocked and speechless at the moment. I can't believe that I am about to be a dad.

Her labor went pretty smoothly. She had some pain but not a lot until she was getting ready to push. I held her hand and did my best to encourage her. I can't even describe the moment that I heard my daughter's first cry. It was the most beautiful sound ever.

After she was placed on Audrey's chest she was handed to me. It was the best feeling in the world to hold her in my arms. I instantly loved her. My baby girl.

"Audrey, thank you so much." I said as I looked at her. "This is the best gift in the world."

CHAPTER 7

Justin's POV

I am headed to this hospital dreading what's about to happen. Yesterday Audrey had her baby and the DNA test was done. In about an hour the results should be ready. I want to be there when Max gets the results because he is going to be hurt.

I'm not just being an asshole and talking out of my ass, this is something that I know. When Audrey left Max I did a small investigation on her and what I found was horrible. She had been sleeping with several men. I also heard that she did this same thing to her ex, left him days before the wedding. I didn't even know that she was engaged during college.

She was seen around town going in and out of clubs with different guys. When I spoke with some people they said that she bragged about how she used Max being in love with her to get spoiled and that she never had any intentions on ever being with him seriously.

She talked about him and his family. I was told that she seemed to get off on the fact that she crushed him and the part that pissed me off the most is that she did it for no reason at all. Some people said that they asked her why she did it and she said, 'because I can," and that's why I hate the bitch.

When I get to the hospital I don't immediately go into the room. I stayed in the hall and just watched Max through the window and it sucked. He is leaning back with the little baby laying on his chest. He looks so happy and content. It makes me feel bad that he is going to be hurt but the truth is always better.

Ring Ring

Me: Harris

Caller: Hi, Mr.Harris. This is Lauri with the lab. We have those results for you.

Me: Okay. You can bring them up to the mother's room.

I ended the call before knocking on the door. "Hey." I said as I walked in.

"Hey, Justin. What are you doing here? I didn't know that you were coming." Max said.

"Yeah, I wanted to be here when you got the results."

I sat behind him on the window seal and waited for the person from the lab to come in. About ten minutes later there was a knock on the door and then a lady entered the room.

"Hello. I need to deliver DNA testing results to Audrey Thomas and Maximo umm Maximo Knight." She said Max's name slowly, no doubt recognizing his name. When she looked up and her eyes widened at the sight of him.

She handed the papers over to both of them but Max handed his to me. I opened it and just as I suspected Max is not the father of the baby. I showed him the paper and he instantly had tears in his eyes. He looked at Audrey looking hurt and broken and she was just sitting there. She hadn't even opened the letter so she obviously knew the truth the whole time.

"Why, Audrey?" Max asked her.

This bitch just shrugged her shoulders and said, "I needed stuff for my baby and I knew that you would be so quick to take care of the needs if you believed the baby was yours. Simple. I didn't originally plan on pinning her on you but when you saw me it just made sense."

It took everything in me not to act a fool in that hospital. I don't hit women but somebody needs to whoop Audrey's ass. How can someone be so heartless?

"But I had to beg you to be a part of the baby's life." he said with his eyebrows furrowed.

"It was a part of the plan to make it seem believable. I knew that you would do whatever it took to be in her life if you thought that she was yours. Justin just ruined my long term plans by telling you to get a dna test but at least I got everything that she needs for a while."

"Why would you do this? What have I ever done to you?" he asked her.

"Nothing. I just did it because I can." she said as if fucking this man's life over was a meaningless game to her.

Max sat there for a minute just holding that baby and staring at her with tears in his eyes. Then he stood up and placed the baby in her little bed. He leaned over and kissed her on her head. He whispered something to her that I couldn't hear and then he walked out of the door.

I walked out behind him. He was walking kind of fast so I had to hurry so that I could catch up with him. By the time I caught up with him he was getting in the back of his SUV. I went to the other side and climbed in next to him.

He stared for a minute before leaning his head back. "Fuck. How could I be so fucking stupid?" he asked as he looked at me. Then I watched as my best friend broke down. I just held onto him. There was nothing that I could say.

"Jensen, take us to his place. I will send for my car later." I said.

"Yes, sir." he said with sad eyes. Jensen knows how hard Max took it when that bitch left him but this hurt was different. I can tell that he already loved that baby and now he can't have her.

Max's POV

I never thought that I would have a day that was worse than when Audrey left, but I was wrong. This day is by far the worst of my life. Nothing could have prepared me for the heartache that I feel.

The moment that I saw that little baby I loved her and now I can't have her. I am not her father. She was just a pawn in her mother's endless games.

I don't know why but I never thought that Audrey was lying about this. I know that she left me but this is a baby. I wouldn't have thought that she would lie on and use her own baby.

Fuck, this is hard. I stared at that little girl before I left because I knew that it would be the last time that I saw her. I laid her in her little bed and whispered, "I hope your mom changes for you. I will always love you" before walking out of there for good.

At that moment Audrey was dead to me. There would never be any coming back from this. She could have done anything else to me but this.

By the time I reached the car I was barely holding it together so when I got in I just broke down. I cried not only for my heartbreak and the loss of a baby that I thought was mine, but I cried because I had no idea what would happen to that baby.

I will never see her again and based on how Audrey has been so manipulative I don't know if she would be a good mother to her. She has barely even touched her since she was born. The only affection that she has felt came from me.

When we made it to my place I got out of the car and just walked in a daze trying to keep myself together. I found myself walking towards the nursery just zoned out until I heard Justin calling my name.

"Max...Max, where are you going?" he asked and I didn't say a word. I just kept walking until I stopped in front of the door. "No, Max. I'm not letting you go in there. It's only going to hurt more. No."

"I just need to see it one more time, that's

it." I said to him and as much as I could tell that he didn't want to, he nodded his head. I walked around that nursery and looked at every single thing that I had laid out for my baby. Her little blanket and coming home outfit was still laid across her crib.

I took in every single thing and took it in mentally before leaving that room. "Get rid of it." I said firmly.

"W-What?" Justin asked confusingly.

"Get rid of it all. Donate it or do whatever the fuck you want to but I want it out of my house by morning." I said as I walked away.

I was done with this shit. All I know is that another woman won't get a chance to hurt me ever again.

CHAPTER 8

Max's POV (several months later)

It's been months now since the baby was born. I thankfully have not seen or heard from Audrey. At first it hurt for a long time but I eventually just realized that sitting in a room thinking about it wasn't going to help me at all.

I had fallen in love with the idea of being that little girl's father but the reality of it is that I wasn't and there was nothing that I could do about it. So, I made the choice to move the hell on and get over it. Life goes on.

My life is somewhat back to normal now. I say somewhat because I have made some changes in my life that I think are for the better.

I don't allow people in anymore and it works for me. I keep professional relationships only. On the rare occasion that I am with a woman I make it clear that there will be nothing coming from us sleeping together. Sex and every now and again a dinner is all that I can offer, take it or leave it because I could care less.

I don't really hang out much unless it's with my family or Justin. We have gotten back to our usual gatherings and dinners. Tonight is an exception though. Tonight is the annual Scandalous party for my company. It is an appreciation party that we throw every year for our employees.

We really let our hair down at these parties. While it is usually used for mingling there is a dress requirement that requires everyone to bring out their inner sexy. It's all in good fun and it is always a good time.

Justin of course came up with the idea after our second year being over the company. He thought since I worked them so hard, and I do, that they deserve a time to enjoy themselves and each other.

I will be wearing an all black suit as usual. This is mainly for our employees so I don't get too worked up over what to wear although I do enjoy seeing everyone else dressed up.

When the party starts I do my usual speech. I thank everyone, talk about the progress of the year, and of course announce their holiday bonuses. Then I walked around to greet some people before I started drinking and wasn't able to remember a damn thing.

My first stop is to visit my parents and the guests that they invited. It will probably be one big annoying ass moment just like last year's party and the holiday parties that my mother throws. They always look at me with pity and the ladies always hug me like I am a little kid whose dog just got run over.

"Hey, mom. Hey, dad. Hello, everyone else." I said as I walked up.

"Oh, give me a hug sweetheart. Are you feeling better?" See what I mean.

"I am fine, Miss Lola. I'm not trying to be rude but I do wish that you all will stop asking me that."

You would think that when I say something to them that they would learn to leave it alone but nope. Miss Lola just hugged me tighter causing me to roll my eyes. And already I have had enough of this shit.

"Okay. Well, mom, I spoke, you have seen me, and now I am leaving. The next time that you see me I may not know who you are so have a good night." I said as I walked away.

I headed straight for the bar. If I saw you on the way there I spoke but I wasn't going out of the way. When I got to the bar Justin was already there with a drink in his hand.

"Starting without me?" I asked him.

"I tried to wait but seeing as I ran into both

of our mothers and got the settling down speech I think that I deserve a drink." he groaned.

Justin is the sacrificial lamb. After what happened with Audrey no one speaks to me about settling down anymore so he gets it from both of our mothers. It irritates the hell out of him too.

"So, what exactly did they say to get you drinking?" he asked knowingly.

"Well, your mama is still on that shit where she thinks that she needs to coo me every time she sees me." I said with a smirk.

We started talking about a whole lot of nothing honestly while we drank until it was interrupted. "Justin, come dance with me." We turned around to see my little sister.

"I'm talking, Lindsey." Justin said. I have no idea why he even bothered to deny her.

"Does it look like I care?" Lindsey said and I chuckled.

"You know that she isn't going to leave you alone until you dance with her." I said. He shook his head and then headed to the dance floor.

My little sister and her never ending crush on Justin. I'm not even sure if you can call it a crush. And I don't know why he doesn't just admit that he likes her too. It's annoying as shit to watch him pretend not to.

I stayed at the bar drinking and watching everyone dance. I was enjoying relaxing until I looked over and saw an unwanted guest coming towards me.

"What the hell are you doing here?" I asked.

Justin's POV

Ugh...Lindsey has pulled me on the dance floor once again. You know if I wanted to find a date at an event I would never be able to because this is how she is. She is always demanding my attention.

I have to admit though that she looks absolutely beautiful tonight, just as she usually does. "You look beautiful tonight, Lindsey, but why are you such a little brat?" I asked her with a smirk.

"Call me whatever you want as long as you call me yours." she said to me with a smirk.

"Lindsey, you know that I can't and I don't want any trouble out of you at all tonight, Lin."

She sighed and just leaned into me while we danced. I hate when she gets like this but I love it too because she does feel good in my arms. Maybe one day I will be able to hold her all the time, that's if she doesn't give up on me.

We were still dancing three songs later when

I looked up and saw that Max had a look of shock and anger. I followed his line of sight and got pissed off too. I rushed over and stood almost in front of him.

"What the hell are you doing here, Audrey?" I asked angrily.

"My date invited me of course." she said with a smirk.

"Justin?" Lindsey called my name and I knew what she wanted but I am trying not to make a scene in front of everyone.

"Not yet, Lin."

"Audrey, you have no right to be here. You know damn well that you aren't invited to my company events." Max said.

"Why not? Can't a single mother enjoy herself?" she said with a smirk.

"Now?" Lindsey asked.

"No."

"Audrey, do you remember what I said to you the day that you showed up pregnant? Well, that wasn't a threat. That was a promise. You have three seconds to get the fuck up out of here."

"Oh really." she said while looking at me causing me to chuckle. I guess she doesn't think that I am serious.

"1...2...Lindsey." I commanded and before I could get her whole name out she was on Audrey's ass like a wild damn animal.

"Justin, stop her." Max said in a panic. He knows damn well that I am the only one that can hold her back, but I'm not going to because I warned the bitch.

"Not yet." I said through gritted teeth.

"JUSTIN." my mom and Mama Mary yelled in unison. Fuck. They act like she doesn't fucking deserve it.

"Alright. Come on, my little firecracker." I said as I grabbed Lindsey but she was still trying to get to Audrey. "Lin, that's enough." I said firmly, causing her to calm down and relax.

"Whoever she belongs to, come collect your bitch." I said and this guy walked up. "Monday I want a valid reason for why she was brought here to cause drama and if there isn't one you're fired." I said to him.

I turned around to check on Max. I know that he is probably pissed but he wasn't showing any emotion. "You good?" I asked.

"I'm good. She isn't about to ruin my night. Fuck her. Let's party."

CHAPTER 9

Justin's POV (two and a half years later)

A lot has changed within the last couple of years. When I say a lot I mean a lot of Max has changed. He isn't the same person anymore and I am not sure how I feel about it. I know that his family hates it and I also know that his staff does too.

He is still a good friend. He still is a good son and brother. He is still a good boss in terms of financial stability but he is cold with everyone other than his family and me. He doesn't talk to people like he used to.

Growing up and even in adulthood me and Max have always played our roles well. He was always the sweet and caring one. I was the one that was the tough and headstrong one. Max was a very nice person that loved everyone and I only had love for my family, Max, his parents, and of course Lindsey.

But now things are different. He is mean and

cold. He does not give a damn about people. And I know that it all came from that bitch Audrey. The only good thing about him being so firm with everything and everyone is that his business has taken off. How could it not when he leaves no room for error at all? You will be perfect at Knight's Incorporated.

And don't get me started on these women that want him so much just to get their hearts broken. You can have sex or nothing. It sounds so forward but I am telling you that is exactly what he tells them on the date if he actually takes them on a date first.

All I know is I would much rather have the old Max back. I always teased him that he loved people too hard and that he was always so smiley and playful but now I miss it. I miss my friend.

Max's POV

In the last two years or so, my business has been successfully growing. Last year I finally landed the deal that made me a billionaire. It was definitely a proud moment for me. When I took over this business from my father we went from being a smaller business profiting about twenty five million dollars a year to this.

Sure that's a lot of money but being that it's

a family business those profits were split between my grandfather, my father, Lindsey and me. It's a big difference to what the company is profiting now. My personal shares and profits make me a billionaire on my own.

Last year we moved into our new office building that was created as a general space for all of my companies. This was a huge step and improvement for Knight's Incorporated.

With such a growing company we have recently had to hire about thirty new employees that will be coming in next week so my day will be filled with preparations for that. As usual for new employees we will be having a welcome brunch.

Me and my assistant worked throughout the day to ensure that everything was set for next week before heading out for the day.

Just as I am about to leave my phone rings. I looked down to see who was calling and couldn't help but to roll my fucking eyes.

Me: Yes, Lexi

Lexi: Max. Hi.

Me: What do you need?

Lexi: Umm...I'm sorry. I was hoping that you would take me to dinner tonight.

Me: And why would I do that? Didn't we already

have dinner this month?

Lexi: Yes, Max, but I kind of wanted to talk to you about something that is important.

Me: Meet me at Elaine's in twenty minutes.

I ended the call and headed to the restaurant. I wonder what the hell she could want now. If Lexi mentions anything about a relationship this will be her last time seeing me. I am very open with the woman that I am seeing at that moment. They know up front that I am not looking for a relationship.

Lexi mentioned it before but to be honest she wouldn't be my type either way. She tries to act sweet and innocent but I'm not stupid. She moves around to whomever has the most money and wants to fuck her at the moment.

I arrived at the restaurant before she did. I was sitting at the table checking my email when she walked up. "Hey, sweetheart." she said with a cheesy smile.

"Max." I said.

"What?"

"My name is Max, not sweetheart or any other pet name that you want to call me." I said firmly.

"Okay, Max." she said with wide eyes.

"So what did you need to talk to me about?" I asked her.

"Well, I was hoping to talk to you about us actually dating."

"I don't date and you know that"

"Then what are we doing right now, Max?" she asks.

"Having dinner. Well, technically a dinner meeting since you requested my presence. But let's not pretend. You knew on the very first day that me and you would never be in a relationship. Now whatever we were, is done."

"Max, no. I'm sorry. I just...I won't ask again." I just rolled my eyes. This little fake innocent girl act that she is putting on is unnecessary.

"Lexi, it's done. Now enjoy the rest of your meal and Elaine will send me the bill." I said as I left the table.

I have work to do so I don't have time for this shit.

Ava's POV

Oh my God. I am so excited right now. In one week I will be moving to New York. I have always dreamed of this since I can remember and thankfully I am able to.

I was born and raised in a small town a little outside of Phoenix. New York has always been my place to dream about so I made a plan to move there as soon as I was able to.

I worked hard in high school so that I could earn as much scholarship money as I could. I knew that if my schooling was free then I had a better chance of getting to New York during my timeline.

I started working right at 16 and saved every penny that I could. During college I worked hard during school and I also worked a full time job. I know that New York is expensive to live in so I wanted to save as much as I could.

Thanks to my lovely parents who supported me on this, I was able to save up almost all of my income from the past six years.

The best part of it all came just a couple of weeks ago. I had applied for several jobs in New York. I know that it takes a lot of experience working with big companies so I was a little hesitant to apply for some of the jobs but I stepped out on faith anyway.

Thanks to my Godfather's business I did have some experience working in a corporate setting and plus I had my college records to help me. I was contacted about a position with Knight's Incorporated. I almost died and went to heaven when I got that phone call.

Working for them would be an amazing opportunity. My Godfather told me all about the company and I was impressed. I just have to make sure that I work extremely hard because the owner is a perfectionist from what I heard.

Knock Knock

"Hey, sweetheart. What are you doing?" my mom asks as she enters my room.

"Just packing a few more things. I know that you all are going to send a few boxes but I wanted to make sure that I have enough stuff with me until they get there." I said.

"Oh, my baby. I can't believe that you are going to be over 2,000 miles away from me." she said with tears in her eyes.

"Oh, mom. Don't do that. You're going to make me sad." I said with a pout.

"I don't want to make you sad. It's just, you are so shy sometimes. I am just worried. I am so proud of you though for sticking with your plan."

"Thank you, mom." I said as I hugged her.

"Alright, girly, come on down. Everyone is here to wish you well."

When we made it downstairs I literally saw my whole family sitting in the yard. Everyone came to have dinner with us and to give me gifts before I left. I am so thankful for my family because they blessed me with quite a bit to help me along the way.

"So, little cousin, make sure you enjoy yourself and not just work." my cousin Taylor said as she pulled me to the side to talk.

"Well, how about I get settled first before I start doing your form of enjoyment."

"Ava, at some point you have to stop being the nice girl and have some fun. Enjoy New York and find a man while you're at it. Then maybe you can finally get some." She said and I scoffed.

"Everyone's mind isn't always on sex like yours."

"Most people's mind is but I'm not telling you that you need to always think about it. Shit you are a total virgin. I mean you don't know shit." she said and I rolled my eyes.

"I know what you're getting at and I still don't see anything wrong with it. I want my first orgasm to be from the man that I will give my virginity to." I shrugged.

"Well, hopefully he comes soon before you become an old lonely woman."

Despite my crazy cousin it turned out to be a really good evening. My family can be a bit much but I wouldn't trade them for anything. After the busy evening I was so happy to just sit back and relax.

Tomorrow is my moving day. New York, here I come.

CHAPTER 10

Still Ava's POV

When I arrived in New York I could not believe it. I was finally here. Moving to an unfamiliar city can be a bit scary but I am determined to make it work here. Thankfully the company that I will be working for assigns other employees to help anyone that is moving in from out of state.

My assigned helper is a guy by the name of Tyler Jones. Apparently he is from Arizona too which is why I was paired up with him.

Tyler has been a huge help already. He helped me to find a place that isn't far from the job and has emailed me tips and suggestions. When I spoke with him this past week he also informed me that he will be meeting me at the airport.

Stepping off of the plane was so exciting. I couldn't believe that I was finally here after working so hard to achieve my goal. I went to grab my luggages and headed out of the airport to meet Tyler. I took a look around but I didn't initially see him so I sat on the bench and waited.

"Miss Ava Ross, it's a pleasure to meet you in person." I hear a voice say so I turn my head and see that it's Tyler.

"Hi, Tyler. It's nice to meet you in person as well." I said with a small smile.

"Let me get your bags so that we can head to your new place."

"Thank you, Tyler." I said as we walked to his car.

The ride was a little long because of the New York traffic. That's definitely something that I am going to have to get used to. It was a nice ride though because I was able to get to know Tyler. I feel like me and him can become really great friends.

When we finally arrived at my new place I was shocked at how beautiful everything is. The pictures that he showed me doesn't do this place justice at all. We headed upstairs and I was stunned.

"Tyler, there is no way that this apartment is $3200 a month. How?" I asked confusingly. It's a beautiful apartment in downtown Manhattan that is just a twenty minute walk from my job.

"Well, the actual cost is $4200 but the boss owns it so employees that are coming in from out of state get a housing incentive for the first year.

He actually owns several apartment buildings but since you said that you wouldn't be using a car right away this is the best option."

"Wow...That's kind of amazing. This is pretty cool." I was amazed at how good it was going so far. Tyler gave me another list of helpful numbers and addresses. He also recommended that for right now I get some groceries delivered instead of going out since I don't know anyone.

"Alright. I will see you in a week at your welcome meeting. If you need anything between now and then just give me a call." he said as he was leaving.

"Thank you for everything, Tyler." I said before locking up.

The first thing that I did was call my mom and dad on Facetime. I don't think that the phone rang a whole two times before my mom answered the phone squealing like a little school girl.

Mom: Hey, my baby.

Me: Hey, mom. Where is dad?

Mom: Hold on. Let me get him.

Dad: Hey, sweetheart. How was your flight?

Me: My flight was amazing. I wanted you all to see my apartment. It is so amazing.

I walked around and showed them everything. They were really impressed with it and looked just as shocked as I was when I first walked in.

Mom: Wow. That's a very nice place. I would have thought that you would have to pay more.

Me: Well, according to Tyler this building is owned by Mr.Knight so new employees get a housing incentive for the first year. I didn't know that at first but that is amazing.

Mom: That's great, honey. I can't wait to hear more about your job when you actually start. Make sure that you check in very often.

Me: I will. I love you guys.

Dad: Love you too, sweetheart.

Mom: Love you, honey. Be good.

After ending the call with my parents I got started on arranging my apartment the way I wanted it. Thanks to Tyler my furniture and other items that I needed had been delivered. The furniture was already set up so I just needed to decorate and organize everything. Since I have a whole week to get settled I decide to stop and wait until later to finish.

I ordered some food and sat down to start planning out my week. Once I was done I ordered groceries and everything else that I thought that I may need. Then I settled down and watched tv until I fell asleep.

The rest of my week was full of preparations for the upcoming Monday. I did a little shopping, I organized my apartment, did some sightseeing to get to know the area, and got plenty of rest. And now it is finally Monday morning and it's time for me to head into my new job.

I decided to keep it simple since this was just a meeting and we will not be working today. I dressed in a blue dress with little yellow flowers on it. I wore some cute little flats and I tied my hair up in a messy bun.

I am not really into a lot of makeup but I put a little something on my lips. I wore my good luck necklace and a pair of earrings. I hope to make a good impression on the people that I will be working with and maybe meet a few nice people to hang out with.

I took a deep breath and headed out of the door. The walk to my job was not bad at all. It didn't take me long even though the streets were crowded.

Arriving at the building I started to get nervous. The place is huge and there are a lot of people going in since it is early morning. I take a few deep breaths and head inside.

Walking in I have to of course go through a security check. I was directed towards a table that had information for the new hires before being directed to the room where the welcome breakfast is being held.

When I walked into the room I was a little overwhelmed. There were maybe about 60 to 80 people in there. In the email it was said that our assigned helpers will be in attendance so I figured that I would wait towards the entrance until I can find Tyler.

"Hey, Ava. Did you find everything okay?" Tyler asked.

"Hey. Yes I did. I was just waiting for you. I wasn't expecting there to be so many people." I said nervously.

"It will be fine. The company hired quite a few people at one time. Come on. Let's grab our seats. We are up front."

We were soon served with a nice breakfast. A short time later there was an announcement that came in saying that in a moment Mr.Knight will be speaking. I took a look at the stage to see if I could spot my new boss and was surprised to see that he was looking right at me.

When I first looked at him I had to remind myself to breathe. The man is an extremely handsome man and although I didn't know a thing about him, just looking at him made my body heat up. I had never experienced such an attraction to anyone and I didn't know what to do with it. I was stuck. I should have looked away but I couldn't.

He didn't seem like he wanted to look away either but then suddenly he started to look so mean, cold, or irritated maybe. He was looking at me as if I did something wrong but I don't know what it could be when I just got into the room and we don't even know each other. I couldn't have possibly done anything wrong already.

Soon he came up and gave us a welcome speech and let us know some important things about the company as well as explaining the tour that we will receive.

After eating and mingling we paired up in groups for our tour. About halfway through a girl came over to us and told Tyler that he has been reassigned because him and I will be working in different departments and they thought that it would be best if I had a female helper.

"But I see that other women have male helpers." I said confusingly.

"I'm sorry. I was just told that I am your new helper. I'm Cammy." she said with a smile.

"Hi, Cammy." I said hesitantly. I really like Tyler and was hoping that we could be friends. He has helped me so much.

"No worries, Ava. If you need anything I can still help you along with Cammy and we can still hang out as friends." Tyler said with a smile.

CHAPTER 11

Max's POV(From that morning)

Knock Knock

"The welcome breakfast will be starting in ten minutes, Sir." my assistant said.

"I will be out in a minute." I said. I finished up a couple of emails and then headed downstairs to the meeting room.

When I walked in I sat at the back of the stage because I like to look around and see how everyone mixes together. In order for a company to be successful there has to be communication and positive energy.

As my eyes slid past one of the front tables I had to do a double take. The girl sitting there caught my attention instantly. Fuck. She is gorgeous. She looks so innocent and sweet. And I instantly knew that I wanted her. I want her bad just by looking at her.

She started looking around before looking up

to the stage and noticing me looking at her. Our eyes meet and the only thing that I can think of is she is mine.

As I am watching her I see that she keeps talking to the guy next to her which means that he is with her so he must be her helper. I don't fucking like it.

"Justin, who is this at the front table?" I asked him.

"Umm, let me check my list...Her name is Ava Ross and the guy is Tyler Jones. He is her helper."

"And why was she paired with a man?" I asked as I looked at him.

He runs background checks on everyone and pairs them with the best fit for them as their helper. However, there is no way that my Ava is going to have a man as a helper.

"In my notes it says that they are from the same state. Their hometowns are maybe an hour apart. I figured having someone that is from the same area would be good."

"Reassign him and give her another helper."

"Why? They seem to get along pretty well from what I can see."

"Yeah and that's the fucking problem. Put her with that girl Cammy. I trust her." I said firmly.

"Max?" Justin said as he looked confused.

"Just do it, Justin, and I want it done now." I said firmly. I don't know why but I feel extremely possessive over Ava and I don't even fucking know her. All I know is that I don't want another man so close to her.

I stood up and walked to the front of the stage so that I could give my speech. I'm talking to the audience but I can't keep my eyes off of her. I have never been so attracted to someone in my life, not even Audrey. It feels like, I don't know, like my soul is attracted to her.

After my speech everyone went their separate ways for their private tours. I headed back to my office before I do something stupid like actually talking to Ava. I can't do that.

I walked into my office and closed the door but it was pushed back open by Justin. I sat down at my desk and got back to work. I can tell that he is staring at me so I pause. "Yes, Justin. What do you need?" I asked.

"What's going on with you, Max?"

"Nothing is going on."

"Max, you forget that I know you. So there is no point in lying. There has to be a reason that you wanted Ava's helper changed. There are other women that are paired with male helpers and you didn't say a damn word."

I took a deep breath to try and calm my nerves.

"I don't know, Justin. I feel like...like...I feel like she is mine." I said honestly. His eyes went wide.

"So you like her?" he asked.

"No...I mean yes, but it's not like that. I really feel like she is mine. One look at her and I feel like not only me but my soul wants her. I...I don't understand it."

"Max, what do you mean you don't understand? That's normal for people to feel when they meet someone special."

"Not for me. I can't feel that for her because I can't have her."

"Why not? Because you were hurt? Max, you let one situation change who you are. You used to be happy, fun, and loving. You don't even live your life anymore. Don't you think that you deserve to be happy?"

"Justin, just look after Ava, okay. I need to get back to work." I said. I didn't know how to respond to what he said so I just didn't.

Ava's POV

Walking around the building I am a little intimidated by how big it is. I will definitely have to learn my way around. Cammy is really nice although I still think that I would have preferred to keep my same helper. He has helped me so much so far and now I'm going to have to get used to someone else.

"And that's everything. When you come in tomorrow morning this will be your office." Cammy said.

"What do you mean? I thought that I was going to start on one of the lower floors in a different department."

"I really don't know. I can get Justin to maybe explain it to you. I was just told that this would be your office when you were in the bathroom...Oh, there is he now." she said and I turned around to see a guy walking towards us.

"Hey, Justin. This is Ava. She was a little confused about her position. She was told that she would start on one of the lower levels but I just showed her the office here that was assigned to her." Cammy said.

"Hey, Ava. Yes, we reassigned you to this floor. After reviewing all of your school records and work history we feel like you are experienced enough to work on our upper level projects."

"Wow. I am speechless. Thank you. That's amazing." I said with excitement.

"No problem. So this is where you will come in the morning. We will have a meeting tomorrow in the conference room at 9 am for assignments. See you then." Justin said as he was leaving.

"Cammy, oh my gosh. How is this possible? That's so amazing." I was having a hard time controlling my excitement. This opportunity was by far better than any of the other places that I had applied at.

"It doesn't matter how it happened. Just enjoy it...Enjoy your evening because the work starts tomorrow. If you need anything before then let me know." she said.

We exchanged numbers and then I left for the day. I can't wait to call and give my parents the awesome news. As soon as I walked in the door I called my mom.

Mom: Hey. I wasn't expecting to hear from you until later. Everything okay?

Me: Hey, mom. Calm down. Everything is fine.

Mom: Oh okay. How was the meeting today?

Me: Well, the great news is my position was changed. I will actually be working on the upper floor on bigger projects.

Mom: Oh wow. That's great. Congratulations, sweetheart.

Me: The other news is that I have a new helper. Her name is Cammy and she seems nice but I would have preferred to keep Tyler.

Mom: Oh. Why did they change it?

Me: Me and Cammy were told that it was best for me to have a female instead of a male but it doesn't make sense. Other ladies had male helpers.

Mom: Well, who made the decision? Was it Mr.Knight?

Me: I'm not sure. I didn't meet Mr.Knight personally. I only saw him in the meeting room and he looked mad. I was talking to Tyler and looked up to see him looking at us with anger. And then not long after that Cammy came.

Mom: Maybe Mr.Knight likes my sweet little Ava and he didn't want Tyler close to you.

Me: Mom, you're talking nonsense. The man might be the most handsome man that I have ever seen but he doesn't even know me. Now it's time for me to hang up. Bye.

I ended the call because she is always trying to set me up or get me to date someone. What she never realized is that it wasn't that I didn't want to date but no one wanted to date the nerdy girl that was always working and studying.

That's why as of today I have never had a boyfriend. I know that it's sad but it's true. I'm not proud of it but I am proud that I never gave in to peer pressure and that I kept working towards my goals. Now look at me. I am in New York like

I always planned and with a great job. It's only up from here.

CHAPTER 12

Max's POV

Today will be such a busy day. Of course I have my usual morning meeting with Justin but then we have a company meeting to give the new employees their assignments. I also have two other meetings and some conference calls.

"Morning." Justin said as he came in.

"Morning. Let's get to it because we have a lot of shit to get done." I groaned with displeasure. I need a fucking vacation.

We went through all of our regular categories and got that done. "Is there anything else?" he asked me.

"Yes, actually there is."

"How did Ava get home yesterday?" I asked him.

"She walked. She lives in one of your buildings of course. It's like a twenty minute walk from here."

I think about it for a minute and I do not want her walking. It's New York. The streets are always crowded and she doesn't know the area.

"Assign Jensen as her driver. Let Drew know that he will be with me from now on."

"And what if she doesn't want that?"

"Then convince her. She doesn't know New York or anyone here. It's not optional."

"Max, this could all be solved if you just introduced yourself to her like a regular person."

"Justin, I'm not doing that. I can not have her but I will take care of her and make sure that she is safe. That's it. Now let me get back to work. I have another meeting in an hour."

I worked on some accounts until it was time to head to the meeting. When I got there everyone was already seated. Walking into the room my eyes immediately went to Ava. She looked so beautiful sitting there.

I got a little lost in my thoughts of her until I heard someone clearing their throat. I looked over and it was Justin. Fuck, Max. Get yourself together.

I reeled in my stupid thoughts and got the meeting started. Two hours later we were walking out and I headed back into my office to finish out this crazy day.

Hours went by and I ended up having lunch

at my desk while working because I am so busy. I got so caught up in my work that I didn't realize how late it was getting until I received a text from Justin.

Ping -*Hey. Ava got home just fine. Jensen said that she was a little surprised but she wasn't upset or anything-*

-*Thanks, Justin. Keep me updated on how things are going with her.-*

Ping -*I will but if you stop torturing yourself you can find out for yourself.-*

It really irritates me when he tries to fix my life but at the same time he doesn't take his own advice.

-*I will stop torturing myself when you do the same.-*

Ping -*What is that supposed to mean?-*

I don't know if he thinks that I am stupid or not but I have known for a long time that he is in love with my sister and she is just as in love with him too. He won't do anything about it but sure lets act like I am the only one with a problem.

-Exactly what I said.-

Ava's POV

I don't think that I have ever been this excited for anything but I am extremely excited for today. It is my official first day on the job. I get up and shower quickly so that I won't be late. It took me a while to figure out what I am going to wear but I decided on gray pants, a white button down shirt, and a black sweater.

I do some light make-up. I put my hair in a bun and then I take a long look in the mirror. I think I look pretty good. Sure I am not the best person for fashion but I am satisfied with it. I take one deep breath to relax my mind. Alright, Ava. Let's go conquer this day.

I get started on my walk and twenty minutes later I arrive at the building. I don't mind the walk but it is so crowded in the morning.

Heading upstairs I go straight to my little office. The meeting where I will get my first assignment doesn't start for over an hour so I take some things out of my bag that I brought for my office.

Knock Knock

"Morning. How are you?" Cammy asked as she

walked into my office.

"Morning, Cammy. I am doing great. I am excited for today."

"That's great. I'm glad that you're excited. Hold on to that excitement when Mr.Knight gets to fussing about assignments...So there is about thirty minutes before the meeting but we should head down. Mr.Knight likes us to get there early. Trust me. You do not want to be late for a meeting." she groaned.

"Noted. And yes, let's go ahead and head to the conference room." I said as I stood up and walked around my desk.

I was a little nervous about the meeting. This will be my first official meeting and assignment with the company. I just want to do well and make a name for myself.

As we enter the room there are several people that are already here. They looked just as nervous as me and some of them were not new employees. That did nothing for my comfort or confidence.

Everyone was chatting and then suddenly everyone went silent. I thought that it was weird until I looked up and saw Mr.Knight and that guy Justin walking into the room.

When he entered I was so nervous because he was looking right at me. As nervous as I was though I couldn't take my eyes off of him either. It was like we were both stuck until Justin cleared his throat.

Jeez. What the heck is this? Why am I feeling such an attraction to this man that I do not know? I have never felt this way about anyone. It's so weird. Finally the meeting is over and I am thankful because my head is a bit cloudy over Mr.Knight.

I headed back to my office with Cammy right behind me. As soon as we were behind closed doors she looked at me with this huge smile.

"Umm, missy...I think Mr.Knight may have a thing for our little shy Ava." she wiggled her eyebrows as I rolled my eyes.

"Oh God, Cammy. Why would you say that?"

"I mean it makes sense. He couldn't keep his eyes off of you when he walked into the room. And placing me as your helper. Me and Mr.Knight have a very trusting relationship since I have worked here so long. I have never seen him even give a woman a second look after...Nevermind."

"After what, Cammy?"

I shouldn't say. It's not my story to tell."

"Okay." I said but I really wished that she would have finished her sentence because I was dying to know more about him even though I shouldn't. Maybe I will look him up later.

"Alright, I will leave you to your tasks. Do you understand what you are supposed to do?" She asked.

"Yes, I think I have it. It doesn't seem bad." I shrugged.

"Good. Well, I am headed to my office. If you need anything just let me know." she said as she left.

I made it through my day way better than I thought I would. I was surprised but it went well. When it was time to go I packed up my bag and double checked my computer. Just as I am about to head out there is a knock at my door.

When I opened it there was a man standing there. "Hi." I said.

"Hello, Miss Ava. My name is Jensen and I will be your driver from now on."

"Uumm...I don't understand. How are you my driver? Is this something that's a part of the new employee's package because no one has said anything to me?" I asked with confusion.

"I'm not sure about the details, Miss Ava. I was just told that I will be your personal driver from now on. No matter if it's to take you to work or to the store I am to assist you with that."

"Umm...I'm not sure if I am in need of a driver. It's just a short walk for me."

"Please, Miss Ava. You are under no circumstances to walk around New York alone. I will take you wherever you need to go. It's my job, ma'am."

I really don't know why I am getting a driver but I guess if it's his job I guess it's okay. "Alright, Jensen. Thank you." I managed to say, although I still didn't understand.

CHAPTER 13

Max's POV (months later)

Tonight is our annual Scandalous party and I can't wait. This is the first time that I have ever been so anxious to go to one of these parties and the only reason is Ava. I can't wait to see her all dressed up tonight. I have no idea what she is wearing but Jensen did say that he took her and Cammy to pick out something.

It's been months since Ava started working for my company. I somehow have managed to avoid saying a lot to her but it's fucking driving me insane every fucking day. My thoughts and dreams are all consumed by her.

I honestly don't know how much longer I can keep this up but I am trying my best. I just haven't been in a relationship in so long but I could never do the casual thing with Ava. If I was to be with her I would want all of her and would want to give her all of me.

Justin of course keeps trying to convince me

to forget about the past and talk to Ava but I just...I don't know. Sometimes I want to so badly but then I always talk myself out of it. Regardless though I have kept my word to take care of Ava since the day that I have met her. I am able to see her every day in the office and for now that is enough for me.

Ping- *Mr.Knight, I will be arriving in 10 minutes, Sir.-*

-Thanks, Drew, I will be down by then.-

    I look in the mirror and take a quick look at myself. I went with the usual all black attire so I look about the same as last year. With a shrug I head downstairs and out of the door to where my driver is parked.

    When I arrived at the party everyone was already seated and the room was a little dim. I didn't initially see Ava so I decided to look for her later. I walked up on the stage and gave my usual speech. Everyone was excited because the Christmas bonuses increased this year. After that it was time to mingle and party.

    Me and Justin grabbed us a drink before going over to see our moms. He said that he needed one because he knew that they would be bothering him once again about settling down. Five seconds in they proved that he wasn't wrong because that's exactly what they did as soon as we walked over.

"Hey, boys. Max, your speech was wonderful. Justin...I was really hoping that you would have someone on your arm this year, son." Miss Lola said.

"Me too. I just knew that this would be the year, Son. What are you waiting for?" my mom said.

I just shook my head. I am so glad that it's not me that they worry with this shit. Justin hates it because he hears this shit everytime that they are together which is often.

We talked to them for quite a while. We were just about to walk away when I saw Ava and I instantly got pissed off. What the fuck was Cammy thinking with this fucking dress that she picked for Ava? It's too fucking revealing.

I know that she is supposed to dress sexy but fuck. I am so fucking pissed. I didn't realize how hard I was squeezing my glass until it shattered and my mother screamed a little.

"Max, what happened?" Justin asked. He looked over to where I was looking and moved slightly in front of me. "Fuck...Max, you need to calm down." I know that I need to but fuck I can't. Every fucking man in here is looking at her.

Before I knew it I was walking to her and I instinctively moved her body in front of mine. "Ava...What are you wearing?" I asked slowly because I am trying to stay calm.

"S-Sir...I..I...Cammy s-said that this is what I should wear to this kind of p-party." She stuttered because she was so nervous.

I took a deep breath because I don't want her to think that I am mad at her and she looks a little afraid right now too so I knew that I needed to relax. How was I going to relax? I have no fucking clue because with Ava I feel like a fucking caveman that wants to throw her over my shoulder and take her out of here.

Ava's POV (a few hours earlier)

Ping- *I'm headed up-*

A couple of minutes later there is a knock on the door. I quickly opened it. "Hey, Cammy." I greeted her with excitement.

"Hey girl. Are you ready to get dressed?"

"Honestly, hell no I'm not." I said to her and she laughed but I don't think that it's funny.

I did not want to go to this party at all but I was told that it was mandatory for all employees. The problem isn't necessarily the party but it's what I am wearing to it. Cammy picked out my dress based off of the previous years and God I have never worn something like this before.

The dress is mostly black. My whole right side

and back are black. I also have black long sleeves. But the dress is low cut and from the breast area to the bottom of the whole left side is covered in diamond like crystals. The dress is knee length but there are openings on the dress starting just under my breast and going down the whole left side. Right at the top of my left thigh it opens and that's where the dress ends on that side. Did I mention that it's also tight? If not let me say that it's skin tight.

It is very sexy and a little too revealing for me. However, Cammy insisted that this was how everyone else will be dressed. I am sure that I will pass out from embarrassment before the night is over.

After I got dressed, I hesitantly stepped out into the living room and Cammy screamed. "OH MY GOD...Ava, you look AMAZING." I smiled because I was so happy that she liked it.

"Really? Is it that nice?"

"Girl, YES. Mr.Knight is going to LOVE IT." she squealed.

"Cammy, stop with that." I said as I shook my head.

This girl and her ideas. She has been swearing since day one that Mr.Knight is attracted to me. You should have seen her smirking when she found out that I had a personal driver.

I have to admit that I was extremely surprised to know that I was the only employee with a personal driver. My response to her is always how could he like me if he never says a word to me.

Am I attracted to him? Absolutely. The man makes me wet just from looking at him but the truth is I don't think that he is interested because he has literally said the bare minimum to me since the first day that I started at the company. Cammy keeps telling me that there are reasons as to why he is that way but she refuses to comment on it any further so whatever.

I have not said a word to her about how attracted I am to Mr.Knight. I wanted to make sure that I looked nice tonight so that he would like my dress but I am nervous that it's a bit too much.

Ring Ring

Me: Hello, Jensen.

Jensen: Hello, Miss Ava. I am downstairs.

Me: Okay, we will be right down.

"Okay, girl. Let's get going." I said to Cammy. We headed down and then we were on our way to the venue. When we arrived I begged Cammy to sit towards the back. I was super nervous and wasn't ready to be seen yet.

A few minutes later Mr.Knight comes up and

FIGHTING LOVE

gives a speech. I have to admit that I didn't even hear half of it because I was too busy staring at him and how handsome he was dressed in all black.

Once the speech was over and it was time for everyone to mingle, Cammy had to make me get up because I didn't want everyone to see my dress. Oh God, I don't want to do this. Why in the world is this the theme for the party anyway? I hate it.

Me and Cammy stopped walking to talk to someone. A few minutes later I heard a small scream and looked over to see Mr.Knight holding a shattered glass. He looks angry, very angry and the scary part is he was looking at me.

He starts walking towards me and I don't know why but the look on his face makes me want to run. When he reaches me he places his body in front of mine as if to block people from seeing me.

"Ava...What are you wearing?" He asked me slowly like he was trying to stay calm.

"S-Sir...I..I...Cammy s-said that this is w-what I should wear to this kind of p-party." I stuttered because I was nervous and I didn't know what else to say or do.

He took a deep breath like he was trying to calm himself. I am embarrassed to say that I am a little afraid right now. I can feel my eyes starting to water because I don't know what's wrong and he looks so angry. Justin walked up and whispered something to him.

He looked into my eyes quickly and then took a deep breath. He took off his suit jacket and put it on me. "Wear this and do not take it off at all. Do you understand?" he said firmly.

"Y-yes, Sir." I mumbled while rapidly nodding my head. Then him and Justin turned around and he walked away.

CHAPTER 14

Still Ava's POV

"So, you still want to tell me that he doesn't like you." Cammy said but I couldn't respond. I was still trying to figure out what the hell happened. I just made my way back to my table and took my seat. I sat there with my head slightly down trying not to look at people.

A little while later Justin came to the table. "Ava, Mr.Knight would like to have a word with you." he said. I nodded my head and then stood up to follow him. God, I hope that I am not going to get fired.

He walked me to this lounging room and left me there. Mr.Knight was standing on the other side of the room. "Ava, come here." he said firmly. I slowly walked over to him, looking anywhere but directly at him. I was so nervous.

"Ava, are you okay?" he asked me and I nodded my head. "I'm...I am sorry for losing my temper. I...was just...surprised to see you...wearing that."

he groaned.

"I...I'm s-sorry." I said, my voice barely a whisper.

"You don't have anything to be sorry for. I should have kept control." he groaned again.

"I am...still...sorry...Cammy thought that y-you may l-like this dress." I mumbled. I didn't want to tell him that but I wanted him to know that it wasn't my fault that I was wearing this.

"Don't apologize. It's the theme of the party. Cammy is right. You do look beautiful in it. I just..." he paused and took a deep breath. "Ava, I just...damn this is hard."

I felt bad for him but I don't know why. I don't know what's going on but he had a painful look in his eyes. "What's hard?"

"Telling you that I have feelings for you." he said, causing my eyes to go wide.

"You like me?"

"I don't mean like, I meant what I said. The first day that I saw you it already felt like more than just attraction. I felt like my whole soul was connected to you." he said leaving me speechless for a moment.

I was also a bit confused. "And why is that painful for you?" I asked him. I am surprised at how comfortable I am talking to him about this.

"What do you mean?"

"I saw pain in your eyes when you said that."

"Because I...relationships haven't been my thing for a while." he said and I couldn't stop myself from asking him why. I thought about some of the things that Cammy said every now and then and concluded that something must have happened to him in his personal life at some point.

"That's a story for another time, Ava...I just know that I have been suppressing my feelings for you for months and I really can't hide them anymore." Umm, I have no idea what I am supposed to say to that. This man is extremely handsome and he is a freaking billionaire for God's sake and he is standing here saying that he has feelings for me.

How? Why? Is this some kind of crazy joke? I have never dated anyone and as far as I know there is no one that has wanted to date me and all of a sudden he wants me. I am shocked.

"Ava." He called my name and lifted my chin with his finger.

"Hmm?" I hummed.

"You're mine." he said to me with pure possessiveness. I again was speechless. I don't know why but I feel like I want to be his so I managed to nod my head a little bit and he smiled.

That was the first time that I have ever seen him smile and it was beautiful.

"Good girl...Well, I guess that we need to get back in there but stay with me okay." he said and I again nodded my head. He grabbed my hand and pulled me back inside. I was nervous and shy about everyone seeing us this way but I don't think that he would let me go. Not with what I have on anyway.

I wasn't wrong either. He didn't let me go or let anyone get close to me at all as long as we were at that party. God, this is embarrassing.

Max's POV

I know that I have lost my fucking mind. I tried hard not to let Ava know about my feelings for her but that fucking dress just wouldn't let me not approach her. She belongs to me and I don't want anyone looking at her that way.

When I was talking to her I was trying so hard not to show my anger but I was livid. I can't believe that Cammy picked that out for her. I wanted to say something to her but then Justin came and whispered to me, telling me that I needed to step out and calm down because I was scaring Ava to the point of her having tears in her eyes.

Fuck, I didn't realize that I was that fucking

mad. I took off my suit jacket and put it on her to cover her up. Then we stepped out into another room and of course he had a mouth full to say.

"Max, so you didn't know that this would happen at some point? You thought that you could hold it back forever. You need to reel in your anger and apologize to Ava. You scared the shit out of her in there."

"I know, Justin. Fuck...I just couldn't control it...Man, what the fuck am I going to do now?"

"Talk to her, Max. Give yourself a chance to be happy. Damn don't you think that you deserve it. Are you going to let that bitch ruin your life forever?" At this point he was yelling because he was getting angry with me.

I took a deep breath and closed my eyes for a moment and thought about what he said. I really don't have a choice but to talk to her so I may as well let her know how I feel. "Go and bring her to me. I will wait right here."

When Ava came into the room I could tell that she was scared. I was pissed at myself for making her feel that way. I don't know what is wrong with me when it comes to Ava. I don't usually lose control of myself like that about anything.

As hard as it was and as much as I was trying to talk myself against it I took Justin's advice and told her how I felt. She didn't say much and I can tell that she is still nervous but as long as I get her everything will be fine.

We are now back out at the party and we are walking hand and hand. I don't want her out of my sight at all. My first stop is the bar because I need to grab me a drink to calm my fucking nerves. "Would you like a drink, Ava?" I asked her.

"Maybe just some wine, Mr.knight." she mumbled.

"Max."

"S-Sir?"

"Call me Max."

"Okay, M-Max." she said nervously.

I grabbed both of our drinks and then we headed over to where Justin and Lindsey were. A part of me didn't even want to go over there but I knew that I needed to let them know that I was okay and I also wanted to tell them that we would be leaving.

"Are you calm now?" Justin asked, causing me to chuckle. I am sure that he was just as shocked as I was. There has only been a few times in my life that I got that mad. I try to avoid anger because I lose myself quickly when I do get that mad.

"Ava, this is my sister Lindsey. Lindsey, this is my angel Ava." I said.

"Hello." Ava said shyly. Lindsey didn't say

anything which pissed me the fuck off. I won't tolerate anyone being rude to her.

"Just wanted to let you know that we would be leaving...Come on, my angel." I said as I grabbed her hand and walked away.

CHAPTER 15

Ava's POV

Umm...Somebody pinch me because I have got to be dreaming. This man...Mr.Knight...Maximo Knight is claiming me. I know that I should be offended that he told me that I was his instead of asking but I'm not for some reason. It excites me.

He seems sweet but when his sister didn't speak to me he looked angry and scary. I didn't know what to say or do but thankfully he said that we were leaving. I was happy because I was too nervous to be there any longer.

He pulled me to the truck and helped me in. When he got in with me Jensen looked back with this huge smile. "Finally," he said and Max laughed while I looked shocked. Apparently everyone knew that he liked me but me.

He held my hand the whole way to my place and his other arm was wrapped tightly around my waist. I instinctively snuggled into him. What exactly is wrong with me and why am I so comfortable with this man?

When we got to my place Max got out with me. "Jensen, I will be back down soon. Maybe thirty minutes." he said. Crap. He is coming into my place.

When we made it into my apartment I mentally thanked myself for cleaning up earlier this morning. Max sat down on the couch and pulled me into his lap. I was so nervous. I didn't know what to do, where to look, or what to say.

He took a deep breath. "My sweet girl Ava...I have waited a long time to hold you in my arms." he said as he held me close to his chest.

He held me like that for a while without saying a word. It was comfortable though. I actually found myself about to drift off to sleep until he sat me up and looked deep into my eyes. He grabbed the back of my neck, pulled me into him, and kissed me. Oh my God. He kissed me. I can't believe it.

As he kisses me he starts rubbing his hands down my back and legs. Oh God. My body is starting to heat up and feel things. I might need to get off of him because I can feel moisture in between my legs.

All thoughts of being a virgin have left me because all I can think about is what he could do to me. The way that he kissed me made me wonder how he would kiss me between my legs.

My mind is so cloudy right now. I have never felt this way. I needed to get control of myself so I reluctantly pulled back. "M-Max." I said softly and then I stopped and just put my head down. I didn't want to upset him.

"It's okay. I better go anyway before I lose control again." He said with a smirk. "I will see you tomorrow sometime, okay...Good night, baby." he said as he walked out of the door. I literally almost passed the heck out. Whoa.

Ping- *So, am I still coming back to your place tonight or are you stuck under Mr.Knight?-*

-Oh my God, Cammy. Why would you say that? I'm sorry that I forgot you. I'm sending Jensen back to get you. Be looking for him.-

I picked up the phone and called Jensen. This is so embarrassing. How could I completely forget that she was with me? Thankfully he didn't laugh at my pain and had no problems going back to pick her up.

Not long after Cammy arrived with her teasing me. "Okay, girl. Spill the beans."

Max's POV

Leaving my little baby was hard as fuck but if I stayed there any longer I was definitely going to be doing things that I had no business doing, not yet anyway. I got Jensen to take me back to the party. These things usually don't end for a few more hours. I just left because I wanted to have a little alone time with Ava.

"Back so soon. I thought you would have surely tried to make up for lost time." Justin teased.

"Shut up, Justin. I don't want to rush her. Hell, I already scared the fuck out of her tonight."

"Yeah you did do that." he shook his head.

"And where is your little trouble maker?"

"I already talked to her. Don't go acting crazy."

"Mhm." I hummed.

"You have some explaining to do, son." my mom said as she walked up. I knew that this was coming. I mean I did lose my fucking mind in front of every damn body.

"So how long have you been with this woman?" my mom asked me.

"Physically or mentally?" Justin said with a smirk.

"Don't be an ass, Justin, because I could easily ask you the same thing." I said to him.

I reluctantly tell them everything about Ava. Of course they would like to meet her but I'm not letting them yet. I just got her so for now I am going to be selfish with her and plus I don't want anyone giving her shit because of what happened with Audrey. That's what my sister was doing by not speaking to her and I won't have that shit at all.

"Anyway, I just came back for a little bit to talk to you all since I suddenly left. You all enjoy the party because I am leaving."

I headed home for the night. I wasn't going to be able to enjoy that party because all I could think about was Ava and that damn dress. Now that she is mine I am going to have a hard time moving slowly. I had to talk myself out of calling her or going back over to her place.

When morning came I got up early because I was dying to see Ava. Now that she knows how I feel I can't help but to want to be around her. I need to make up for lost time. I quickly showered and got dressed. I am going to pick up some breakfast and go over to Ava's so that we can talk.

As I am walking out of the door I see Justin getting out of his car. "What are you doing here so early?" I asked him.

"I have some updates about the hotel construction and we have an emergency meeting in an hour."

"Fuck, man." I said before turning around and heading to my office.

"Where were you headed anyway?"

"To see Ava." The asshole smirked. "Justin, I don't have time for your shit today. Just come on so that we can get started."

Justin and I got to work. The issues with the hotel construction turned out to be one big ass issue after another. It's more difficult dealing with these things when the construction site is not only out of this state but also out of the country.

One meeting turned into six. Reviewing emails turned into redrafting some paperwork. And on top of all of that I had to make some changes to a few things. It was one big ass headache and a whole lot of work.

"Ah fuck. I'm glad that is over with. We are going to have to go over there soon." I said to Justin.

"Yeah we probably should head out there as soon as we can."

"Yeah, I will check my schedule and see when we can head out."

"Well, let's go find something to eat."

"Another time. I'm going to see Ava." I said as I stood up to leave.

"This late?" he asked with his eyebrows

furrowed. For the first time today I checked my watch. Fuck, how the hell did I not realized how late it had gotten?

"Fuck, I didn't realized we worked for that long. I told Ava that I would come see her today." I said as I grabbed my phone to call her but I didn't get an answer.

CHAPTER 16

Ava's POV (from that morning)

When I woke up my mind quickly went back to last night. I am still so shocked at what happened at the party and definitely what happened when we came back to my place.

When Cammy came over we spent half of the night talking before we fell asleep. I wanted to talk to Max again but he hasn't given me his number and much to my disappointment he didn't call or text me. He did say that he would see me today though so I can't wait for that.

God, I must be crazy to be so excited over a man that I have been with for practically two minutes.

"And let me guess, you are over there smiling about Mr.Knight." Cammy said, scaring the heck out of me.

"You scared me. I didn't even know that you were awake."

"Yeah, yeah. So, what are we doing today?"

"Well...Max said that he was going to come over so." I said with a wince.

"Oh, I get it. I get it. Girlfriend has a man now so I can't get all of the weekend time." Cammy said, causing me to blush.

"So what time is he coming over?" she asked.

"I have no idea. He left after the kiss and we haven't talked." I shrugged.

"Okay. Well, let's have breakfast and then I will head home."

We headed to the kitchen to make breakfast. We ate while she teased me some more and then she headed out. As soon as she left I thought about calling my mom and telling her that she too was right about Max but I decided to wait.

This is just too new and I wouldn't want to tell her about him until me and him had a chance to talk. So, I decided to get up so that I could shower and get dressed. I don't want to be in my night clothes when he comes.

I put on a cute little dark gray casual dress. I pull my hair back in a straight ponytail. I think I look cute but it's not too obvious that I tried to look nice for him. Now hopefully Max thinks it also.

Since I have nothing else to do today I grab a blanket and snuggle up on the couch. The holiday movies have started so I can spend the day doing this and that's exactly what I do.

Hours passed and I still didn't hear anything from Max. I figured maybe he was coming a little later. I decided to go ahead and order dinner. I ordered enough for two just in case he was here when it arrived.

My dinner arrived a little while later. I ate and since it was late I decided to get ready for work tomorrow. Maybe Max was drinking or something and woke up this morning realizing his mistake. I should have known better than to think that someone like him would be interested in me.

I am disappointed but it is what it is. It's not like I'm not used to being single. I just hope that it's not awkward when we are at work but then again I barely see him. The only problem is since tomorrow is Monday we will be having our regular strategy meeting.

Oh well, it's not like I can avoid it. Since it is getting late I take my shower and head to bed. A good night's rest is definitely needed.

The next morning when I wake up I quickly dress and head to my office. I felt a little awkward riding with Jensen now so I tried not to say much.

When I arrived at the office I tried my best not to be seen by many people. I went to my private office and worked on a few things before it was time for the morning meeting.

Knock Knock

"Hey, girl. Ready to go to the meeting?" Cammy asked as she walked into the room.

"Sure."

We always head to the meetings together. Walking into the conference room I try to sit as far away from where Max sits as possible.

I felt his presence when he walked into the room but I didn't dare to look his way. I didn't want to make eye contact with him and I didn't want him to know that my thoughts were only of him. I just gotta make it through this meeting and I will be good.

Max's POV

I am rushing into work this morning because I want to see Ava. I do have a lot of shit to do but I need to make some time to explain why she didn't hear from me like she expected to.

My intention was to go straight to her office when I made it to the building but I was told that one of my investors was on hold and had been waiting for my arrival.

By the time that call ended it was time for me to meet with Justin which took longer than I would have liked it to. After that I had no time to stop at Ava's office before the meeting. I had to head there now.

When I walked in I immediately noticed her but she was sitting at the other end of the table and didn't even look my way. I was thinking that maybe she was mad about last night. I get started with the meeting and she still does not look up to me and that irritates me.

I try to ignore it but I can't. I stop in the middle of the meeting and walk down to her. I grab her chair and drag it all the way to the front so that she can sit next to me. She looks shocked but she will be alright. I ignore the rest of the shocked faces and get back to my meeting now that I am a little more relaxed.

I finished the meeting as quickly as possible. When it was over everyone stood up to leave including Ava but I pulled her back down in her seat. She still wouldn't fucking look at me.

I sighed as I looked at her. I hope that she hasn't changed her mind about being mine because there is no way in hell am I letting her go.

"Morning, Ava." I said softly.

"Morning." she mumbled.

"Ava, I apologize about…" I started but she cut me off.

"You don't have to apologize. I understand. I

just don't want things to be awkward." she said and it confused me.

"What do you mean?"

"Y-you made a mistake and realized that you didn't like me. It's okay." What the fuck is she talking about?

"Ava, is that what you think?" I asked her and she finally looked up to me.

"Yes."

"Come here, Ava." I said as I pulled her onto my lap. "You are mine, Ava. You need to understand that now because it's never going to change." I told her firmly but she didn't say anything. "Ava, do you understand?"

"Y-yes."

"I apologize to you about yesterday. I really did want to see you but Justin came by and we got busy with work. Time slipped away and I just didn't realize how late it was. I didn't mean to stand you up."

"Okay."

I leaned in and kissed her. "You forgive me?" I asked.

"Yes of course." she said with a smile.

"Good. Now come on. We are leaving for the day."

CHAPTER 17

Ava's POV

Okay so I completely read that wrong. I just assumed that this wouldn't mean anything to him. I mean look at him and look at me. The man can have any woman that he wants and he decides to have me. Shocking.

When we left the conference room we walked hand in hand down to the car. "Jensen, take us to Ava's." Max said.

I was nervous, real nervous. We were together for only about 30 minutes the other night and I swear it made me want to do things that I had never thought about before.

When we got to my place just like the other night Max pulled me into his lap. "So, how do you feel about all of this?" he asked me.

"Umm...Honestly, I feel weird because I am happy about it and I feel very comfortable with you."

"Why does it feel weird?" he asked with his eyebrows furrowed with confusion.

"Because...I," I stopped because I felt embarrassed. I try to look away but he turns my face back to him.

"Tell me, Ava." he said firmly.

"Because I have never dated anyone before." I said slowly. His eyes went wide first before a smirk appeared on his face.

"I love that because it means that you will forever be only mine." I couldn't help but to blush at that.

"I am glad that you are comfortable with me though because after wanting you so bad for months...I don't know if I can hold back." he said before kissing me.

Our kiss started out slow but just like the other day it got heated very fast. All I kept thinking is I want him to touch me and my body the way that he did the other night. I don't know if it makes me a whore or not but at the moment I don't care.

I have never had anyone touching on my body and it feels so amazing. I shift on his lap so that I am straddling him. I can feel his hard bulge under me. I moved a little bit hoping that he would get the hint that I wanted him to touch me and he did.

He started rubbing up my legs. "Mmm." I moaned into our kiss.

"Fuck, Ava. You moaning like that makes me want to do things to you that you are not ready for."

Yeah, I may not be ready to lose my virginity but I feel like I am ready for something. As of today I have never even played with my own self.

Max starts back kissing me. He trailed kisses down my neck and it is really turning me on. "Oh God." I moan and he stops and looks me in my eyes.

"Does this feel good to you?" he asked me as he teased me by rubbing on my thighs getting close to my sensitive spots but not quite there.

"Mhm. Better than anything I have felt before." I moaned.

"Even better than when you touch your pussy?" He asked me and I tensed a little. What was I supposed to say? I wasn't sure but then I didn't have to say anything because he guessed it right.

"Ava, have you ever had an orgasm?"

Max's POV

I swear that I am not trying to move too fast with Ava. It is hard as fuck though when she is looking at me the way she is. I can tell that she wants me to touch her even if we aren't ready to have sex.

When I started rubbing on her she started moaning as if it was the most amazing feeling and it made me wonder if she had even had an orgasm before but I didn't want to ask at first. But when she tensed up at my question I had to ask. "Ava, have you ever had an orgasm?" I asked her and she blushed. That gave me my answer.

The first thing that my sweet girl needs to do is learn what her body can do and feel. "Come on, sweet girl. Let's go to your room." I said as I stood up with her still wrapped around me.

When we got to her room I laid her on the bed. I can tell that she is nervous so I needed to calm her. "Ava, I am not going to have sex with you but I am going to make you cum, okay." I said to her and she nodded her head slowly.

I lifted her dress over her head and unsnapped her bra. She was breathing so hard from being nervous. "Ava, you need to calm down, okay. If you want me to stop at any time, tell me."

I first started rubbing on her breast before bending down and sucking on them. "Oh God, Max." she said as if the feeling shocked her. I kept my assault up on her breast until she was comfortable. Then I reached down and ripped her panties off of her while still sucking on her breast.

I started to rub her little pussy as I leaned up

and kissed her. Fuck...I want her so bad but this isn't about me. She need to know the feeling of her first orgasm before I can even think about fucking her.

"Mmm." she moaned.

"Does that feel good, sweet girl?"

"Y-yes." she moaned. I can tell that she is getting close so I started back rubbing on one of her breasts.

"M-Max, s-something umm I...I f-feel...I" she doesn't even know what she wants to say. Her mind is going crazy.

"Shh...Baby, relax and let go. Let your body have what it wants. " I whispered to her.

"Ah..Oh, God." she moaned.

"Let go, Ava." I commanded her and she came while screaming my name.

Fuck...The day I have her is going to be so fucking amazing. I can't wait to suck the juice from her wet pussy. "How was that, sweet girl?" I asked her.

"It was good." she said slowly. Her eyes looked hazy. I climbed all the way in bed with her and pulled her into my arms.

I had to laugh a little at her because she was falling asleep. Her little first orgasm wore her out. Once I was sure she was knocked out I called Justin and asked him to bring my laptop so that I could work while she was sleeping.

Of course when he got there he had a lot of shit to say. "Where is Ava?" he asked.

"Shut the fuck up. She is sleeping. Don't be loud." I said with a glare.

"Damn, you put her to sleep already?" He is such an ass.

"Justin, just leave. I will communicate with you over the phone. Get out." I said as I pushed him.

I got started on my work and actually got quite a bit done. After a while I figured that I should wake her up so I had Jensen bring us some lunch. Once it arrived I went to wake my sweet girl up.

She was still knocked out and in the same position that I left her. I rubbed her cheek. "Sweet girl, it's time to get up...Ava...Get up you need to eat." She finally opened her eyes and smiled. "Come on so we can eat."

"Mmm...Maybe I should shower first."

CHAPTER 18

Ava's POV

Max giving me my first orgasm was amazing. That feeling was a feeling that I can not fully describe. My only thoughts were how in the hell did I get to the age of 22 without having an orgasm. I wish that I would have been felt that.

Now that I have, I want to feel it again. It also makes me wonder what it would be like to have sex. I mean if it feels that good just for him to rub his hand down there I bet that it feels better to have actual sex.

The surprising part is how tired I was afterwards. I was knocked out until Max came and woke me up.

Now that I have had my shower I head out to the living room so that we can eat. When I enter the room he is sitting back on his phone. I slowly walked in hoping that things won't be awkward and thankfully it wasn't.

We ate lunch and had a nice conversation. We talked about a lot of things and got to know each other more. He stayed a little while longer but ended up leaving in the evening to take care of some important work.

As soon as he was out of the door I decided to call mom. I know what I said the other day but I can't hold it any longer. Now would be a good time anyway since dad is still at the office. The phone barely rang before she picked it up.

Mom: Hey, baby. I didn't hear from you yesterday. I was going to call you when I thought you were off. Why are you off so early?

Me: Hey, mom. Well, the reason that I am off is kind of a long story.

Mom: I've got time.

I took a breath and proceeded to fill her in on everything that has happened between me and Max. Well, except for what we did earlier. For a few minutes she didn't say anything and that kind of made me nervous. Mom wasn't the type to hold back her opinion.

Me: Mom?

Mom: Yes, I am here. I am just a little shocked. I do

recall telling you though that I thought he may like you.

Me: Yes you sure did.

Mom: Well, if you like him I am happy for you.

Me: But? I feel a but coming on.

Mom: It's not what you're thinking. I was going to say but know what you are dealing with. His world is different from yours. I know people in that world and it's tough. People are evil, liars, manipulators, and let's not forget whores. Don't always react to what you hear and if you do see or hear something you take that up with him in private. Don't give them the satisfaction. And if a problem ever does arrive you handle it. You are sweet like your father but you are my child too. Remember that.

Me: Thanks, mom. I just wanted you to know okay. I will talk to you tomorrow.

I am thankful for my mom's advice. She knows how people can be. My aunt dated a guy that was wealthy and she went through a lot. She decided to walk away from the relationship. She spent years heartbroken because she really did love the guy. She just couldn't deal with his world so she left. That's something that I don't want to do unless he actually gives me a reason to. I am happy to see where this goes.

A few weeks passed and things with me and Max are going great. We have gotten into a level of comfort that makes me feel like we have been together longer.

The only challenge that we have had so far or shall I say that I have had so far is a female co-worker named Jessica. She always gives me dirty looks and smart comments when Max isn't around.

I try my best to ignore her but it does bother me sometimes. I am heading to work now and I am sure that today will be no different. I have not told Max about this. I am sure that she won't be the only person that will object to us being together so I figured why make a big deal out of it.

Stepping onto our floor I thankfully was able to make it to my office without running into her so the day is starting off great. I sit down and get to work and realize that I need Max's signature on some documents. I step out of my office and when I get almost to his office I run right into Jessica. I don't know what her problem is with me. I have not done a thing to her.

"Excuse me, whore. Didn't you see that I was headed to Mr.Knight's office first. What, you think because you spend your time being his slut that you can do what you want? I don't know why you think that you are special. Once upon a time I was you, sucking Mr.Knight off and fucking him raw too but he threw me away just like he will you."

"Jessica, if you were going to see him that's fine. I can see him after." I turned around to head to my office. I am so sick of this. I can feel the tears trying to come out because I wonder if what she said is true. That could explain why she hates me so much. Before I could make it to my office I heard Justin call my name and I stopped.

"Ava, Max would like to see you." he said. Crap. I take a deep breath and try to wipe my tears away. I turn around and head into his office. As soon as Max looks at me I can tell that he knows that something is wrong.

Max's POV

As soon as Ava walked into my office I knew that she had been crying but she was trying to hold it in. I stood up and walked over to her.

"Baby, what's wrong? Why are you crying?" I asked her.

"I'm fine."

"You are not fine. What happened?" I asked her and she started holding me tight and she began to shake from crying.

I lifted her and carried her over to the couch

and held her. "Baby, I can't fix it if you don't tell me what's wrong. I need to know what happened." I said to her and she shook her head no.

We sat like that for a few minutes but she still didn't say a word. "Max." Justin said. I looked over to him and he handed me his ear bud and ipad. I watched the video that he showed me and my blood is boiling.

"Ava." I said and she hummed. "Is this the first time that someone has said something like this to you?" I asked her and she said no. "Why didn't you tell me?"

"I don't want any problems. I know that people will try to be mean to me to get to you so I try not to let it bother me...but it does. I'm not usually this upset but what she said bothers me." she said as tears continued to fall from her face.

I looked at Justin and he nodded his head in understanding. I took out my phone and called Cammy to come sit with her. When Cammy arrived I calmed Ava down and then told her that I would be right back.

"Max, don't. It's okay." Ava said.

"Baby, no it's not. And if I am being honest I am kind of pissed that you didn't tell me but I will deal with that later." I said and she gulped.

"Now be a good girl and relax with Cammy." I said before kissing her and walking out.

CHAPTER 19

Max's POV

When I walked out of my office I headed straight to the conference room where I knew that Justin would be waiting with Jessica. I walked in and her eyes went wide.

I didn't waste any time. "So, Jessica, do you have anything that you need to explain to me?" I asked her. I'm trying to see how she is going to explain this shit.

"No, sir. I'm not sure what you mean." she said with her eyebrows furrowed.

"So this is how we are going to play it? I know what you said to Ava. And since you are in violation of your employee contract you're fired."

"Sir, please. It was a mistake. You can't fire me for this." She had the nerve to look as if her feelings were hurt. Did she not think that she would get some kind of consequence for what she did?

"I can do what the fuck I want to do. I am also

firing you for defamation of character which *is* in your contract."

"But, Sir, I didn't do that." She said with fake tears in her eyes.

"You don't think accusing me of sleeping with you or letting you anywhere near my dick is defamation of my character? Because it is. I wouldn't touch you with a fake dick, Jessica. Now you have thirty minutes to leave my fucking building before I have security remove you." I said as I got up and left.

I headed back to my office to check on Ava. "Cammy, let me talk to Ava." I said and she got up and left. I walked over and pulled my angel into my arms. "Okay, now tell me why I wasn't told about this before."

"I just didn't want to start any trouble." she mumbled.

"Ava, don't let that shit happen again. If someone fucks with you I need to know about it. Also, don't ever stand there and let someone speak to you that way because if you do, me and you are going to have a problem. Understand?"

I wasn't trying to be nasty to her but I know how people in this office, especially the women, can be. If she doesn't stand up for herself they will continue to make things hard for her. Ignoring it isn't going to help at all.

"Yes, I understand." she mumbled.

"Okay. Now finish up whatever you need because we are leaving at lunch time for the rest of the day." I said before kissing her and heading to my desk.

I worked until right before it was time to leave and then I walked to Ava's office to get her. I never come to her office because she doesn't want me to, so she was surprised and irritated to see me.

"Max, I was coming in about two minutes. Seriously." she groaned.

"Yes seriously because I obviously need to make sure that everyone knows that you are mine and that you are not to be fucked with." I said and she just huffed.

"You're irritating."

We left the office hand in hand and headed straight for my house where lunch was waiting for us. When we arrived I gave Ava a tour since this was her first time coming over. I would usually go back to her place.

"Your place is nice, Max. Big, but nice and homey." she said.

"I'm glad you like it. I want you to be very comfortable here." What I really wanted to say is because this will be your home soon but I'm gone give her some time.

The last relationship that I was too gone for didn't turn out so well. I don't think Ava would do that but then again I have been wrong before. The difference though is how I feel about Ava. We haven't been dating long but I can actually say that my feelings for her goes beyond anything that I felt for Audrey.

I don't know how to explain it exactly. I did love Audrey when we were together but maybe it's a different form of love because just the thought of not having Ava makes me feel empty.

I don't know why but I feel like I have to possess Ava. Like she is only mine and I want her with me all the time.

We sat down to eat lunch before heading to the living room to relax. Just as always it doesn't take me long to get lost in her. Before I know it she is straddling me and our lips are all over each other.

I started kissing on her neck while reaching under her shirt. I rub on her nipples and I am just about to bend down to suck one of them in my mouth when her fucking phone rings with her mama's face on it.

"I swear your mama is human birth control." I groaned and she laughed before answering her phone. Every single time I am about to have my way with my woman her mother calls.

"Everything ok with your folks?" I asked her after she was done with her call.

"Yeah. They were calling to say that they can't come now. They can't find a good flight."

"Do you want me to send you to them?" I asked her although I would hate to be away from her.

"Umm...I would love to but I don't want to leave you." she said before kissing me. "Now, do what you were doing before my mother called."

Ava's POV

Am I sad about my parents? Yes, but we have been dancing around sexual tension for weeks. As much as I appreciate the orgasms that Max has given me I want more.

There has been plenty of kissing, touching, and groping and while it feels good I want the rest. I want it all. "Max." I said and he hummed. "I umm."

He started kissing me on my neck. "Yes, baby. What do you want? Tell me what you want."

"I want...I want you." I whispered as he continued his assault on my neck.

He stood up with me and walked to the bedroom. When we got there he gently laid me on the bed before he undressed me. He leaned in to kiss me and his lips felt so good on mine.

He moved from my lips and started kissing me down my chest, moving lower and lower until his lips were on my core. He kissed me all around before licking my pussy lips.

"Mmm." I moaned. I never thought this would feel so amazing but it does, God, it does. He kissed and sucked on my clit while rubbing on my nipples and I'm getting there. I can feel it coming.

"Max...Mmm...Max." I moaned as I got lost in this feeling. "Oh...Mmm." I moaned loudly as my body shook from my orgasm.

"You're so beautiful, Angel. I want to kiss and taste every single piece of your beautiful body."

"Max, I can't wait. I want you now." I breathed out to him and he chuckled.

"So impatient today, Angel." he said before taking off his clothes.

"What the...Wow." I said with wide eyes as I got nervous suddenly after seeing his size. "Max."

"I promise you that I won't hurt you. I will be as gentle as you need. You took your birth control, right?" He said and I nodded my head. I started taking birth control right after we started dating. The sexual tension was just too strong so I wanted to be prepared.

"Open up for me, Angel, and relax." he said as he

moved between my legs.

He started rubbing his tip around my entrance and I am trying so hard not to freak out. He leaned in and kissed me before entering me slowly. God, this hurts. "Breathe and relax, baby. Relax and let me in." he whispered.

I tried my best to relax as he continued to enter me until he was completely in and I felt so full. "It's okay. The pain will ease and I will go slow okay." He said to me before kissing me again.

He started slowly moving in and out of me and the more he did the better it felt. "Ava...You feel so good."

"Max...Mmm." I moaned as I was already close to cumming.

"Fuck, baby, you got to hold on. You're squeezing me and I'm trying not to cum." Max groaned.

"I c-can't...I'm going to c-cum." I moaned and I did. I came and he came with me. The feeling was something that I will never forget.

"Fuck. You were squeezing me so tight I couldn't help it." he groaned. "How are you? Are you sore?"

"Yes but I would like to do it again. And even though I am sore, this time I want more. I want you to take me, Max." I said and I swear it was like flipping a switch on him.

He grabbed my hair and turned my head to give him more access to my neck. He started kissing, sucking, and biting all on my neck, face, and lips. He was driving me crazy and I was loving every minute of it.

He entered me hard and fast this time and I couldn't help but to cry out. "Fuck." he groaned as he moved in and out of me.

"Max...Mmm...Max." I moaned.

"Yes, baby...Mmm...Fuck, Ava." he moaned as he continued to give it to me harder and harder. I lost count of how many times I came and just when I thought that I would die from pleasure if I came again, he finally came hard as he groaned, "Fuck, Angel...Mine, Ava. You're fucking mine."

We laid there for a while trying to catch our breath. I couldn't move. I was tired and worn out. The only thing that I wanted to do was sleep so that's what I did. I closed my eyes and drifted off to sleep.

CHAPTER 20

Max's POV

Holy shit. Being with Ava was the best damn thing that I have ever experienced. I'm watching my angel as she closes her eyes and I want to keep this moment forever. I want to keep her here with me always.

I wanted to do nothing but stay in bed with her. However, I have something to take care of so I crawl out of bed and head down to my office to make a phone call. This is going to be awkward as hell but I will do anything for her.

Mrs.Ross: Hello

Me: Hey. How are you doing? This is Maximo Knight.

Her: Oh. Hi, Mr.Knight. How are you?

Me: Please, just call me Max. I was calling because Ava mentioned that you all wouldn't be able to come see her for Christmas. I did offer to send her to you but we kind of wanted to spend our first Christmas together so I was calling to see if I could bring you all here.

Her: Thank you so much for the offer but I wouldn't want you to do that. The flights are just too expensive and they are too long of a wait with the delays. Too inconvenient.

Me: It wouldn't be inconvenient at all, Mrs.Ross. I can send my plane down the morning of Christmas Eve to get you all and it will be ready to take you back whenever you need to get back home. I would really like to do this for Ava if you don't mind.

Her: Umm...Okay. I would love it. Thank you so much. I can't wait to see her.

Me: Okay. Great. I will have a car waiting for you at the airport that will take you to my parents house to wait on Ava.

Her: Okay. See you then.

After talking to her mom I called my mom to make some plans for Christmas Eve. I hope that everything goes as planned and that she is happy.

Since she was asleep I decided to get some work done. Then I headed to the kitchen to see what Ms.Ann was fixing for dinner. I was talking to her when the doorbell rang which shocked me because I wasn't expecting anyone.

"Lindsey, what are you doing here?" I asked as I opened the door.

"Well, hello to you too, big brother." she said as she came in.

"Hey. Now, what are you doing here?" I asked her because I'm sure that it's for some bullshit. She has been a pain in my ass lately.

"Well, mom said that you were home. She also said that you were planning to invite some whore and her parents to Christmas and I was trying to see if you lost your mind." she said.

"Lindsey, I'm going to say this one time and one time only. Don't ever call her that again. I'm not about to explain anything to you. If you have a problem that's your business but if you fuck with Ava then me and you are going to have problems." I said firmly and I mean it.

"I don't trust her."

"It's not her. You don't even know her. You are punishing her for something that had nothing to do with her. I trust her. Isn't that enough? You think that I would let her in after what happened if I didn't trust her?" I said to her but she didn't respond.

I was about to kick her ass out when my watch notified me of a call and I realized that I left my phone in my office. "I will be right back." I said as I went to my office to take the call.

Ava's POV

When I woke up I was genuinely confused for a minute as to where I was until I thought about the moments before I fell asleep. I was so freaking sore. I got up and put on one of Max's shirts before going to look for him.

When I got to the living room I saw that Max isn't in there but his sister is. I know that she doesn't like me so I was just about to turn around when she looked up and saw me.

"Well, if it isn't the person that I wanted to see." she said rudely.

"Hi, Lindsey. How are you?" I asked out of respect for Max.

"I don't know what your plan is with my brother but it's not going to work. A whore like you won't get the chance to get close to him. I will make sure of that."

"Look, you don't have to like me at all but don't call me names and be petty. I haven't done a thing to you. I don't know what your problem is but I don't appreciate you talking to me that way." Not speaking to me at the party was one thing but calling me out of my name and being nasty is downright disrespectful.

"Excuse me? I can talk to you the way I damn well please..." she started to say but I cut her off.

"No you can not. When Max told me that I better not let anyone talk to me this way I assumed that he meant anyone, including you."

"I sure as fuck did. I don't give a fuck who it is. Lindsey, get the fuck out of my house now." Max said as he came around the corner. He was walking towards his sister and he looked pissed so I grabbed him by his arm.

"Max, don't." I said.

Lindsey looked hurt by what Max said and then she turned around and left. I felt bad for her because I can tell that her feelings are hurt. Max was clearly pissed and was very aggressive with her. I'm sure that she isn't used to that kind of reaction from him.

"Max, you shouldn't have kicked her out. That's your sister." I tried to reason with him.

"Ava, I don't give a fuck who it is. When I said no one fucks with you I meant no one."

"Is there a reason that she doesn't like me?"

"Yes, but it has nothing to do with you. It's not your fault and you shouldn't have to pay for other people's mistakes."

"I want to know why, Max. Tell me

why…Please." I said as I looked him in his eyes. I don't know what it is but I can see in his eyes that it isn't good.

"I'm not talking about this right now, Ava." he said firmly after a few moments and I knew to leave it alone.

I wanted to walk over and hold him but before I could he turned around and walked away. I watched him walk to his office and close the door. I stood there for a minute before deciding not to bother him.

I got comfortable on the couch and turned on a Hallmark Christmas movie. I was almost done with the movie and he still hadn't come out.

"Excuse me, Ava." Ms.Ann said.

"Yes." I said as I turned to her.

"Dinner is ready if you would like to go ahead and eat." She gave me an apologetic smile.

"Thank you but I think that I am going to wait on him." I tried to be positive although I wasn't sure how long he would be in this mood.

I finished watching the movie and then I decided to get up and take a shower. I'm not sure why he got so upset but it wasn't my fault. I just wanted him to talk to me and the fact that he got so upset that he disappeared in his office for hours hurts my feelings.

I was in the shower for a while when I heard him come in. I just turned away from him. I didn't know how to feel about any of this.

CHAPTER 21

Max's POV

I know that I was being an asshole to Ava but I was irritated as fuck and not just because of Lindsey or Ava asking me why Lindsey acts that way.

I was more so irritated that when it was brought up that it still affected me. The subject still got under my skin and it pissed me off because I don't want it to. I am happy with my life and I am happy to be with my woman. That shit shouldn't bother me anymore.

When my phone buzzes with a text I see that it's from Justin. I am not surprised at all but whatever.

-You really could have warned me that you upset Lindsey.-

-Keep her from my fucking house with all of that bullshit.-

-Max, that's fucked up. She is your sister.-

-And Ava is my woman and I won't have anyone disrespecting her. Lindsey is your problem, not mine. Now I am done with this shit.-

I think about what I just said to him and then I think about how I was being an asshole to her for something that wasn't her fault. I got up to go to her but she wasn't in the living room so I checked the bedroom.

I could hear the shower running. When I walked into the bathroom she turned away from me. I knew that her feelings were hurt and felt like an asshole for it. I undressed so that I could join her. I slid in behind her and wrapped her in my arms.

"Angel, I'm so sorry for being an asshole. I shouldn't have done that." I whispered to her but she didn't respond so I turned her around to me. "Baby, I'm sorry." I said as I looked into her eyes.

She nodded her head and then I leaned in to kiss her softly. When she kissed me back she did so with need, a need for me. I lifted her up and pressed her back against the shower wall and entered her slowly.

"Mmm." she moaned. I started moving in and out of her hard.

"Fuck, baby." I groaned before leaning in and

sucking on her nipples.

"Max...Ahh...Oh, Max." she moaned as I continued to fuck her.

I needed to be inside of her. I needed to feel her and I wanted to pour out my feelings to her and that's what I did. With every thrust I let her know how much I needed her and how sorry I was for treating her that way.

"Max...I'm going to cum...Mmm." she moaned.

"I'm cumming too, baby...Fuck. I'm cumming." I groaned as I came with her pussy clenching around me.

I kissed her again as I eased out of her. I wanted to tell her so bad that I love her because I do but I didn't. I can't. I don't want to push her or move too fast.

We finished showering before having dinner. Once we were done I left to take Ava home. I hate leaving her every day and I definitely don't want to tonight since I was such an asshole to her but I have some work that I need to get done.

When I got back home I worked until almost morning. Then I laid down and rested for a few hours before getting ready to head to the office.

Ava's POV

Now that the high of being with Max has settled down I started thinking about how I am going to miss my parents. This is my first time being away from them on Christmas and it sucks, but I want to spend this Christmas with Max.

I was hoping that Christmas with him would be perfect but after seeing his sister yesterday I am not so sure. She seems to hate me for something that has nothing to do with me. I hate it but I'm not going to worry about it.

I get dressed for work and I am about to walk out of the door when my phone rings from a number that I don't recognize.

Me: Hello

Unknown Person: Hey. Is this Ava?

Me: Yes. Who is this?

Unknown Person: This is Lindsey. Please don't hang up. I wanted to know if you could meet me for coffee this morning if you don't mind.

Me: I don't think that is a good idea. I am actually headed to work anyway.

Her: Please. I promise that I just want to talk. Please.

I want to tell her to piss off but it's his sister and I don't want him to be away from his family for me. So, I agreed to meet her at the coffee shop across from the office. When I arrived she was already there sitting at a table in the corner. Taking a deep breath I walked over to her.

"Morning." I said as I walked up to the table.

"Good morning, Ava." was all she said. I sat there for a few seconds looking crazy because I wasn't sure what she wanted to meet with me about and I wasn't about to try and guess either.

"I...I asked you to meet me here because I wanted to apologize to you for my behavior. I don't mean to be a bitch. It's just...my brother has been through some terrible situations because of his ex and I didn't want him to go back to that place."

I didn't say anything. I mean I understand not wanting your brother to be hurt again but we are grown and she is acting like an immature kid. I'm not sure what happened with his last relationship but that has nothing to do with me.

"Ava, please. I love my brother, I do. And I realized that my actions are pushing him away. I just want the chance to start over."

"Lindsey, I.."

"What's going on here?" I closed my eyes as I heard his voice. "What's the problem? You still on the bullshit, Lindsey? Can't you just be happy for me?" Max said.

"Max, calm down. She just wanted to talk...Lindsey, I...I think starting over would be great. You're his family. I wouldn't want you all not to get along because of me." I said to her.

"And, Max, I'm sorry for the way that I was acting. I know that I can be a bit much sometimes but I never meant for it to hurt you. I swear." Lindsey said.

And finally all was well between me and his sister. I still want to know what happened but he obviously isn't ready to talk about it and I'm not going to force him.

We headed into work after that. I was in my office when Cammy came in to speak as always. "Mmm. Someone is glowing today." She teased me.

"I am not." At least I don't think I am. Like seriously will everyone know that we left work early yesterday and got nasty. Jeez.

"Yeah, girl, you're totally glowing. Like, got your back blew out glowing. So your day was great yesterday then, huh?" she said and I can't help but to blush.

"God, yes...Yesterday was great except for a minor hiccup with his sister but it's been resolved." I said with wide eyes.

"Oh, no. So, you have felt the wrath of Lindsey? That girl is a force and she doesnt play about her brother."

"Yeah even though I didn't do anything to deserve it but we managed to talk it out this morning. It was hard for me to understand at first because he still hasn't told me about his past relationship." I shrug.

"All I'm gonna say is it was a bad time for him for a while. It's not my place to say otherwise but if it were me I wouldn't want to talk to anyone about it either." she said and I just nodded my head. I guess I should just let it go for now.

We finished our work day and as usual me and Max left together. This has become sort of a routine for us. "Christmas Eve is in two days. Don't forget that we will be at my parents house for dinner that day." Max said.

"Ugh." I groaned.

"What was that?" he asked with his eyebrows furrowed.

"Do you think that it's a good idea? I mean I don't want any problems." I said honestly. I know that me and his sister have put things behind us but Christmas with them is a different thing.

"There won't be any problems. I promise. You are going to love it and plus I have a surprise for you."

"What kind of surprise?"

"Nope. My lips are sealed. You will have to come to dinner to find out." he said with a smirk.

CHAPTER 22

Ava's POV

Waking up on the morning of Christmas Eve alone made me miss my parents. I am supposed to be getting ready to have breakfast with them like we always do before going out and doing some last minute shopping.

Instead I am sulking. I should have asked Max to stay last night. I guess I will call my parents to see what they are doing today.

Mom: Morning, sweetheart.

Me: Morning, mom. I miss you guys.

Mom: I always miss you. Any plans for today?

Me: Yeah. Max is coming to get me tonight but I miss our breakfast. What about you all?

Mom: Nothing this morning. We are having dinner with some new friends later on.

Me: Well, I hope that you enjoy it, mom. Can't wait

to hear all about it. Talk to you later. I just wanted to check in.

Mom: Okay, sweetheart. Have a good day.

I ended the call with mom and decided to go pack me a bag. I don't want to stay here tonight alone so hopefully I will spend the night with Max. A little while later there is a knock at the door and when I answer it Max is standing there.

"Hi. What are you doing here?" I ask with a smile.

"Well, I was hoping to have breakfast with you this morning." he said as he held up two bags of food.

"Is breakfast code for morning sex because if so come on in."

"Sex can definitely be arranged." he said as he came in and put the food down.

"And I know exactly where I want you. Come here." he motioned me over to the side of the couch. "First I want you right here." he said as he pushed me over the side of the couch.

"This is the perfect fucking angle." he said as he pulls my butt on the arm of the couch.

"I'm about upside down." I told him, feeling nervous.

"Yes, and I'm going to be so deep." he said as he took off his clothes, showing his already hard dick.

I thought that he was about to sink into me but I was wrong, so wrong. The next thing I felt was his warm and wet tongue licking on me.

"Oh, Max." I moaned as he licked and sucked all over my pussy giving me that feeling that I now love. Before I know it I am cumming hard but before I can finish he sinks into me.

He moves in and out of me, filling me up with every thrust. "Fuck, Ava." he moaned as he continued to slam into me.

"Deep...So deep." I groaned when he hit a certain spot. "Max, I'm going to cum." I moaned and he stopped.

"Come here and bend over the side." he said and as soon as I did he slid back into me with a groan. "This is how I want it so when your pussy grip me I can bottom out and cum with you." he groaned as he continued to stretch me, giving me the best kind of pain that there is.

This position was so painful and so good at the same time and it didn't take long before I could feel myself about to lose it and I screamed his name. "That's it, baby, squeeze me...I'm cumming with you." he groaned as he emptied himself inside me.

"So good...That was so good." I pant as I try to catch my breath.

"Can we have breakfast now?" he said with a chuckle and I laughed.

"I'm actually really glad that you came over for breakfast. I was starting to feel sad about missing my folks. We usually have breakfast before heading out." I said.

His eyebrows drew together before he spoke. "Maybe we should head to my parents house a little early before dinner."

"That's fine. What should I wear to this dinner? Is it like a dressup thing?" I am nervous. This is my first time ever spending a holiday with anyone but my family.

"No, you don't need to dress up. Wear whatever you like. My mom will probably have on something Christmasy." he shrugged.

"Maybe we can go grab some Christmas sweaters after we eat."

"You can grab you one. I'm not wearing that." He shook his head.

"Ugh, whatever. Well, I would also like to get your parents a gift."

"Why?" he asked with his face scrunched up.

"Because it's the polite thing to do. They are allowing me to spend the holidays with them. I'm thankful." I shake my head. Call it a southern thing but you don't go to someone's house for the holidays empty handed.

We finished up having breakfast before heading out and doing a little shopping. I ended up buying me a Mrs.Claus dress and I got Max a Santa sweater even though he says that he isn't going to wear it.

We bought some presents for his family members and Justin. Now we are headed to get ready before heading over to his parents' house and I am nervous as ever.

When we arrived at his parent's house we were greeted by his mother. This was only my second time seeing her but she was so sweet and very welcoming. As I was talking to her I thought I heard my mom talking. I guess that I miss them more than I thought I did.

We took the presents and placed them under the tree and then we headed to the dining room. The closer that I got to the dining room the more that I thought I heard my mother. I looked at Max with a confused look on my face.

"What's wrong, sweetheart?" he asked.

"I...I must really miss my parents. I thought that I heard my mother. That's ridiculous." I said as I shook my head.

"I wouldn't say that it's ridiculous." Max said and before I could respond we entered the dining room. There sitting at the table was my mom and dad.

I literally ran over to them with tears flowing down my cheeks. "Oh my gosh...What are you doing here?"

"Well, Max wouldn't take no for an answer." my mom said with a chuckle.

I walked back over and hugged Max tight. "Thank you so much even though you could have told me. I've been sad." I said to him.

"It was a surprise. Anything for you, beautiful." Max said with his beautiful smile.

I was so happy for his surprise. I had decided right then and there that I was going to have a nice little surprise for my man tonight. God, I love him.

Wait. Where did that come from? I had never thought of that before. Do I love Max?

I have honestly never thought about it before. I have just been enjoying the ride. Enjoying the times that we share and how amazing it feels to be with him. The more that I think about it the more I realize that I do love Max. I don't want to tell him yet though. Will he think it's crazy since we haven't been together that long?

"So, mom, how long will you all be here? I wish I had of known that you all were coming. I didn't get you anything." I said with a pout.

"Just until the 27th and my gift this year is

getting to see you. I thought that I wouldn't get that chance but thanks to your guy insisting I did." She smirked and gave Max a little wink.

"Yeah, he can definitely insist on something." I said and everyone laughed knowingly.

We had dinner and everyone was getting along great, even me and Lindsey. I was having a good time and enjoying being with my parents but my mind was solely on being with Max later. So much so that I decided to send him a text.

-Babe, I want to go home with you tonight, you know to reward you for being so thoughtful. Can you make an excuse for my parents not to stay with me.-

I watched him check his phone and then he started texting someone. A few minutes later he said, "Mr. and Mrs. Ross, Ava told me how busy this time of year is for you so I hope you don't mind but I booked you at a hotel not too far from her place. I'm sure that you would want to stay with her but I also booked spa treatments and a personal Christmas brunch from the chef. I hope that's okay." he said as if this idea didn't just pop up in his head.

"Oh, sweetheart, you have already done so much for us. You really didn't have to." my mother said.

"Oh, I insist." he said with a smile. About an hour later Max called a driver for my parents and we headed to his house.

"So, bad girl, what's going to be my reward for being such an amazing man?" he asked me.

"Oh, you're just going to have to wait and see."

Cammy has been giving me some tips on how I can please Max. I know that it sounds silly to seek sexual advise but before having sex with Max I knew nothing. I didn't really have girlfriends back home to talk about these things so having Cammy is refreshing. Max is so experienced compared to me. I sure do hope that he is satisfied.

Walking into his place I can barely control myself but I need a little more liquid courage so I headed to the kitchen and grabbed a good bottle of expensive wine with plenty of alcohol. After downing a glass I pour myself another and grab a glass for Max.

When I walked in the living room Max was sitting on the couch doing something on his phone. I walked over to him and politely took the phone from him and replaced it with the glass of wine. Alright, girl. Don't back down now.

CHAPTER 23

Max's POV

I can tell that Ava is nervous as shit right now. She comes into the living room handing me a glass of wine and I'm guessing that she has already drunk hers. She has this look in her eye that tells me that she is feeling hot.

I only wanted to make her happy. I didn't do it to get anything from her but I damn sure am not about to tell her no. She bends over and starts unbuttoning my shirt slowly, too fucking slow if you ask me but I'm guessing that this is apart of her plan so I wait.

She straddles me before leaning in to kiss me. We got lost in the dance that our tongues were doing and when we finally pulled away from each other I saw so much emotion in Ava's eyes, emotions that I haven't seen before.

She leaned back in and covered my mouth with hers before moving to kiss on my neck. I'm loving this little foreplay that she is doing but fuck my dick is about as hard as a brick right now. I need to be inside of her.

Her kisses moved lower and lower as she started unbuttoning my pants. "Close your eyes." she said shyly and I had to ball lips up to keep from laughing at my little shy girl.

She pulled my dick out and covered it with her mouth. "Fuck." I groaned at the contact. Her mouth felt so fucking good as she moved up and down on it. She couldn't take me all the way in so she used her hand to work my shaft.

I couldn't help but to open my eyes and look down at her. The feeling that I had when I watched her take in as much of my dick in her mouth as she could was unexplainable. I had to fight the urge to push further in her mouth.

She moaned and the vibrations were enough to almost make me cum instantly. "Ava…I'm going to cum…You need to move." I tried to warn her but she didn't move away. She continued to suck on me until I was releasing into her mouth and fuck did it feel amazing.

She slowly looked up with a shy smile on her face. "You're fucking amazing, Ava." I said to her as she stood up and undressed herself. I was about to get up but to my surprise she pushed me back down and climbed on me.

"I'm not finished with you yet, Mr.Knight."

she smirked.

She lowered herself on me and slowly started riding me. "Oh, God." she moaned as she moved up and down. "So good…It feels so good."

"Ava." I moaned her name like a prayer from my lips.

She was so fucking wet. "Fuck, Ava…You need to cum…I'm so fucking close." I groaned as I tried not to cum before she could get hers.

I started rubbing one of her nipples while sucking on the other. Then I rubbed her clit with my other hand. "AH…Max…It feels so…Oh, God…Too much." she screamed.

"Just cum, baby. I got you." I whispered to her and her body obeyed me completely as she began to tremble and hold onto me. I came with her and all we could do was sit there, panting, and holding onto each other.

"Fuck…What was the name of that damn wine? I need to buy stock in that shit if it makes you loosen up like that." I said and she laughed as she continued to lay on my chest. My dick was still inside of her and we just sat like that, content on just being together.

Ava's POV

Addicted. I'm freaking addicted. It's the only thing that I can think of to describe how I'm feeling. How in the world do I go from an orgasmless virgin to a sex crazed person? I don't know, but I want it all the time. Especially right now when I have woken up before him and he is laying there with his morning erection like he is just waiting for me to sink onto it.

I wouldn't want to disappoint so that's exactly what I do. As his eyes open he looks shocked at first but it doesn't take him long to match my pace. I ride him and until we both cum and then I politely slide back into my place at his side.

"Fuck...What's gotten into you?...I mean, I'm not complaining at all just so we are clear. Keep that shit up." he says with a chuckle. We relaxed for a minute before having to get up and get our day started. It is Christmas after all.

"What time are you meeting your parents?" Max asked me.

"How would I know? This was all your doing, remember?"

"Well, my woman wanted some of me so I couldn't deny her...They should be finished with everything that I added around 11:30. You can meet them at the hotel then."

"You aren't coming?" I thought that we would spend the whole day together.

"Just thought that you could spend some time with your parents for a few hours. Show them your place and catch up with them and then I will see you a little later, sweet girl. Don't pout or I'm going to suck your lip." he warned me and I huffed.

I got up to get my day started and to get ready before heading to meet my parents. I really was excited to spend some time with them. We went back to my place and enjoyed doing some of our traditions.

My mom prepared us something to eat. We watched a Christmas movie and had a good time. It wasn't like it usually is at home but it was great that we were together.

When evening came my parents informed me that they actually had plans. Apparently Max's parents had invited them to do some things with them and their little circle of friends. I was a little surprised but it left room for Max and I to have some Christmas fun of our own.

He showed me around New York and I can honestly say that there is nothing like Christmas time in New York. Everything was so beautiful and magical. At the end of the night we exchanged gifts. I loved my gift which was a beautiful single pendant diamond necklace and the matching earrings.

The night was so amazingly sweet. By the end of it I had no doubt anymore about the way that I felt about Max. I love him, I really do.

The rest of the week went by with a quickness and soon my parents were off to head back home. Max made them promise to let him know anytime that they wanted to visit and they did. Now it is time to get ready for this New Year's Eve gathering that Max apparently hosts every year at his house.

Dressing up for a small New Year's Eve celebration is not something that I would be doing in my old life. I would more than likely be spending the evening at home having game night with my parents. Thankfully for me I have Cammy to help me get dressed again and boy does she have me looking hot.

We got dressed at my place so Jensen is going to drive us to Max's before he has the rest of the night off. As we are riding we start talking about different things but I am very curious about something.

"So tell me again why you didn't bring a date for tonight." I said. As long as I have known Cammy I have not seen her date not one person. She doesn't even mention anyone.

"It's not that I wouldn't date but I don't think that the person that I want to date wants to date me." she said with a shrug.

"Aha. So there is someone of interest. Is it someone from work?" I asked in a teasing manner but the shock in her eyes tells me that I wasn't wrong. "Okay, spill it. Who is it?"

"Ava...You can't say anything. I mean the guy practically doesn't give me even a glance in passing. I should really just put him out of my mind."

"Okay, but who is this clueless fool?" I asked because Cammy is the real deal.

Cammy is super sweet. She is a loyal person. She is smart and selfless. And let's be honest, my friend is freaking beautiful. Why she chose to do this kind of work when she could easily be a model is beyond me honestly.

"Umm...It's Tyler." she said with a wince and I almost choked on air.

"Oh my God, Cammy. Tyler is a very nice guy. Great choice."

"Yeah except he isn't interested." she shrugs.

Now that her confession has come out I want to have a girls night like right now. We need to talk more but now we are pulling up to Max's place so that's going to have to wait.

We headed in and greeted everyone. I was actually having a great time already. Not long after Lindsey showed up and Max tensed up beside me. I looked at him confusingly for a second. "What's wrong?" I asked him.

"Lindsey is at it again." he groaned.

CHAPTER 24

Ava's POV

"Lindsey, what the hell?" he whisper-yelled.

"Hello to you too, big brother." she said with a smirk.

"Don't act so damn innocent. You know what you are doing." he said and she just brushes past him with her date.

I'm so confused but I don't say anything. I'm just going to watch and see what happens. A few minutes later Justin came from out of the kitchen and he looked visibly angry. When I follow his line of sight I see that he is looking at Lindsey. Hmm.

Nothing happened for a few minutes and then things spiraled. Lindsey kissed her date and the blood literally drained from Justin's face. Max called Lindsey over and he is now looking pissed as well.

"Lindsey, don't fucking do this. Stop playing games." he groaned.

"I'm a single woman. I can date who I want. I

am not playing games." she said to him.

"Yes the fuck you are. That's all you do is play games. That's your fucking life, Lindsey, but that's fine. If you want to play games then we can do that." he said and the fire in his eyes is kind of scary.

A little while later the doorbell rang. "I thought that everyone was here. Who else is coming?" I asked Max and he shrugged but walked towards the door. "Oh, that must be Candace." Justin said.

"Who?" Max asked.

"My date."

"Oh fuck. This is going to be a fucking disaster. Why do y'all have to do this shit today?" Max groaned. I just stood there trying to figure out what the hell was going on.

Justin came back in with his date and introduced her to everyone. I watched as Lindsey's eyes scanned the woman and the way that Justin held her by her waist and smiled at her. During introductions he introduced her as "Max's sister Lindsey." I can tell that he meant it as an insult and that's exactly the way that she took it.

They really acted crazy the whole night. They were really in a battle and at one point I thought that it would go all night until Justin started dancing with his date. They really did seem to be genuinely enjoying each other at that point and then he leaned in and whispered into her ear before kissing on her cheek softly.

I could see the tears form in Lindsey's eyes before she stormed out of the room sobbing. Instead of looking victorious, Justin looked defeated. I moved to go after her but he stopped me. "It's okay, Ava. I need to go. I gotta fix this." he said, looking ashamed.

Max was pissed at both Justin and Lindsey. "They act like fucking children. This was supposed to be a special night for us and they fucking ruined it by being stupid." he groaned. His mood was shitty and I didn't like that.

Max is always sweet. I had never seen this grumpy side of him sitting back, and drinking glasses of whiskey. I stood up and grabbed his hand. "Come with me." I said to him. It would be midnight in a few minutes and I wanted us to be alone. He smiled at me and got right up.

This is him. No matter what happens with him or anyone or anything else he never lets it affect us. He is always everything for me and now I need to be that for him. It can't be easy for him to see his best friend and sister fighting.

At least that's what I thought was wrong with him but I learned that it wasn't when we went to stand on the balcony from his room. "This night was supposed to be special. It's our first fucking time bringing in the year together and I wanted it to be perfect. I wanted our night to be magical. I wanted to dance with you all night and watch you laugh and smile. I wanted to look you in your eyes at midnight and tell you that I love you." he said.

My breath hitched as I heard what he said. Everything else seemed to fade except us. Everything felt distant, even the faint sounds of people counting down. My mind was so cloudy that it didn't register that it was about to be midnight.

"W-what did you say?"

"I said I love you, my Angel." he said just as they counted down to one and the clock struck midnight. He leaned in and kissed me with everything that he had in him and I kissed him with all of me.

When we finally pulled apart he looked me in my eyes. His eyes weren't expecting but they should have been because I have no doubt how I feel about him. "I love you too, Max." A huge grin formed on his face before he leaned in and kissed me again.

At his confession I was feeling really turned on. I wanted him, bad. "You know if it wasn't so cold out here I would let you take me right here."

"Hmm...No worries...By tomorrow evening it will be heated out here and then I want you bent over on the rail. Then I want your legs wrapped around me while I fuck you hard...Now let's head back inside"

When we walked back in I had to stop at the drawer and grab me a clean pair of panties. "What are you doing?" Max asked with his eyebrows furrowed with confusion.

"You think that you can say something like that and I won't spring a leak. I'm freaking soaked." I shook my head as he chuckled.

"Let me see how soaked you are." he said as he lifted my dress and slid his finger over my soaked panties. He instantly groaned and then he slid his finger into my panties. "Fuck. You're dripping." he said in a husky voice.

He lifted my dress before lifting me and sitting me on the dresser. "What are you doing? We have guests." Is he damn crazy?

"Fuck the guests. I need a taste." he said as he slipped a finger in my wet pussy.

"Ahh." I moaned.

He slid it in and out slowly before adding another finger. Then he bent down and started licking my pussy. I was trying not to moan loud but failing miserably. He continued to pleasure me until I was cumming and screaming his name. The orgasm was hard and I was done.

I cleaned up and barely made it back

downstairs. A few of our guests were gone, including Lindsey, Justin, and their dates. We asked everyone what happened but they said that they weren't sure. Everyone was caught up in bringing in the New Year on their own. I guess we will find out tomorrow.

We said goodbye to everyone else and prepared to end the night. We took a not so quick shower before heading to bed but I still needed to be nosy first. "So, explain to me what happened between Justin and Lindsey." I said and Max groaned.

"They're fucking crazy that's what happened… Lindsey has been in love with Justin since she was a kid. When I say in love I mean in love. She wouldn't even date anyone for a long time and when she did it was never anything more than hanging out. She was hell bent on being with Justin and she let everyone know that he is hers."

"So, have they ever dated?"

"Nope. For some reason he just won't date her. I have known for a long time that he is in love with her too and I mean anyone can see the spark between them but nothing. He just goes on pretending that he isn't in love with her. She brought that date tonight to pissed him off but I didn't agree with her doing that. He has never brought a woman around her until tonight, not even to company events or anything like that. It's a bunch of bullshit."

"Well, damn. I'm going to check on her in the morning. We don't even know what happened."

"That's cause somebody was getting their pussy licked." he smirked.

"Yeah, cause somebody was being greedy." I smirked right back at him.

"I couldn't help it. You were very wet. Extremely wet." he groaned.

"Mmm...I'm wet right now too." I smiled as I slid his hand up to feel just how ready I was. He groaned before moving on top of me. We spent the whole night bringing each other to that high over and over again.

When morning came the first thing that I did was call Lindsey.

Her: Hey, Ava. What's up?

Me: Sorry to call so early but we didn't see you when we came back down. I wanted to check on you.

Her: I..umm...I'm okay. Me and Justin talked about everything. We talked about a lot and the reasons that he gave me for not being with me are unbelievable...When Max finds out he's going to be livid.

Me: Oh Lord. With Justin?

Her: No. With my grandfather. He forced him not to be with me. It's a really messed up situation. Is he awake?

Me: No not yet.

Her: Good. Don't say anything. Just let my dad talk to him first.

We talked for a few minutes longer about their crazy situation. I ended the call with "I promise that I won't tell Max anything." After I ended the call I looked up to see Max.

"Babe, why are you looking like that?" I asked, feeling nervous because he looked pissed. I hope that he didn't hear my conversation.

"You promise you won't tell me what?"

CHAPTER 25

Max's POV

The last few months have been fucking hell. I had to deal with all of the bullshit from my family which was a fucking disaster. New Year's Day went from a family dinner to a fucking show down. A showdown that I was in no way about to lose.

I felt bad when I found out that my grandfather was the reason that Justin stayed away from Lindsey. He was never a good grandfather any fucking way. Other than the family business I have nothing to thank him for.

On top of all of that shit Ava got sick. She was sick for weeks. Some weird ass shit that seemed like a bad case of the flu but it wasn't the flu. Whatever it was she was down for weeks trying to recover but thankfully she is finally better.

Even though I never left her side I missed her so much. I missed her being herself and call me selfish but I hate being in the office today because I want to be locked away with her. So much so that I think that we will go away for a few days, just the two of us.

"Ready for the meeting?" Justin asks as he walks into my office.

"Ready as always." I said. We went through our usual routine quickly because I really didn't feel like it. "Anything else I need to plan for?"

"Yes. Me and Ava are going away for a few days."

"Where?" He was smiling hard like he was going.

"I have no fucking clue. I just came up with the idea five minutes before you came in. I just want to be selfish and be only with her for a few days."

"Gotcha. Let me know the details when you have them...And Max." he looked nervous as shit about whatever he was going to say.

"Yeah?"

"Me and Lindsey are going to move in together." he said. What the fuck?

"Why so soon? It hasn't even been that long since you all got together?"

"Max, I have gone years...years being in love with Lindsey and couldn't do a damn thing about it. I never want to be away from her another night. I don't want to waste time and in all honesty I plan to marry her. I know that this has been one big shit show but I have never had any doubts that I wanted to spend the rest of my life with her. My only fear was that she would give up on me before I could actually have her. Thankfully she is a stubborn ass and didn't." he said and we both laughed at that last part.

My sister is indeed stubborn. When she said that Justin would be her husband she meant it and I'm not going to let anyone stand in the way of that. I also now know what Justin had to go through and he did it for me so I have their backs against anyone, I don't give a fuck who it is.

"I understand. Look I'm good with it and if anyone has a problem I got your back. Remember that."

After the meeting I got busy with my work and also busy making plans for me and Ava. By the end of the day I had a plan. In two days we would be leaving and heading to a cabin in Colorado.

I really wasn't sure where I wanted to go but I knew that this was more about us being together privately than it was to do a bunch of fun activities. I wanted us to recharge and connect more than what we already were. She has also been a little moody here and there so maybe she needs some relaxation too.

When we left the office that day we came back to my place together. I have no idea why she won't just move in with me. We don't spend a night away from each other. Either she is at my place or I am at hers. We may as well be under one roof.

We were relaxing and talking when my phone just wouldn't stop going off and I groaned. "This... This is why we are going away for a few days." I said.

"We are?" she asked, looking confused.

"Yes, because I'm tired of this. There is too much going on. I want some time alone with my angel and nothing else." I groaned.

"You're just being grumpy."

"I'm not grumpy."

"You are grumpy. I mean you have a reason to be but it's so not like you." she said. I had no response because she is right, this isn't like me. "Okay, let's talk about something else. Where are we going?"

"Colorado...Just the two of us. I don't care if we do nothing but stay in bed the whole time. I just want some time alone with you."

Thankfully the rest of the night was spent relaxing and relieving my stress in the best way I know, between Ava's legs. Two days later we were boarding my plane and off to Colorado. I was happy as hell for the much needed distraction.

Being away with Ava was the best thing that I could have suggested. Most of the time we never left the cabin. We just enjoyed each other's company. We played pool, watched movies, cooked together, and had lots and lots of sex.

When we did go out it was because Ava wanted to do a little shopping and we tried out a nice restaurant. By the time we were heading home she was pouting because she didn't want to leave. It was the very thing that we needed, rejuvenation and peace.

"I'm going to go back to my place tonight." she said as we were leaving the airport.

"Why? Tired of me?" I teased her.

"No. I'm going to go in to see the doctor in the morning." she said, which alarmed me. I thought that she was feeling better.

"Are you still sick?"

"I'm not sure. I just haven't been feeling well some days and I just wanted to make sure. It's okay." she huffed.

"If you're going to see a doctor you're obviously not okay."

"I'm not a child, Max. The whole time that I was sick you were overbearing and infuriating. I'm just doing a check up."

"Well, I'm going to come with you. If you're sick I want to be with you." I said firmly. I had to tell her and leave no room for arguing. Her little ass has become quite fucking stubborn since she has been hanging around Lindsey's ass. I'm going to have to fix that shit.

"I'm hungry." she groaned and rolled her eyes.

"Ava...Fix the attitude before I fix it for you." I shake my head. Jesus Christ. What has gotten into my Angel?

"What do you want to eat? I will order us something." Yeah cause her moody ass waited until we were pulling up to her apartment to say that she was hungry.

She shrugs her shoulders right before I stepped out of the car. I walked around to open her door and her eyes were glossy. I helped her out and pulled her into my arms.

"What's wrong with my Angel, hm? Why are you so upset?" I asked her because I have no fucking clue. I swear she doesn't act like this at all and I know that I haven't done anything.

"I don't know. I just want to eat and go to bed." she mumbled. I have no idea how we step onto the plane happy as shit and step off and now she is moody and emotional.

"Come on. Let's get my sweet baby to bed then." I kissed her forehead before we went upstairs.

Thankfully after feeding her she took her moody ass to bed but not before clinging to me and crying. "I have no idea why I'm so emotional, Max."

she cried. Shit I don't fucking know either. She has been moody a little but today she was very fucking upset.

Despite her insisting on me going home to get some work done I stayed with her for tonight. Obviously something is wrong and hopefully she will feel better in the morning.

CHAPTER 26

Ava's POV

It took some convincing but I got Max to go into work. He had meetings that he didn't need to cancel since we are just getting back from our trip. We did kind of leave in the middle of a work week. Other than that though I just really wanted to go to the doctor by myself.

I don't know what's wrong with me but I have been a mess emotionally for no reason. I am going to ask the doctor for a recommendation for a therapist and I didn't want Max to freak out about it.

Thankfully when I called my doctor this morning they were able to give me an early appointment so now I am sitting in the lobby waiting for my name to be called. I just hope that nothing is seriously wrong with me.

"Ava Ross."

"That's me...Thank you." I said as I walked to

the back.

"So, Ava, what brings you in today?" Dr.Gray asked. I proceeded to tell her everything that has been going on including the embarrassing emotional drama from the night before.

"Okay...We are going to take some blood and urine. We will run some tests and see what we can find. No worries. We will figure it out." she said but the look on her face suggested that she possibly already knew what was wrong with me which made me nervous.

I don't know how long I expected it to take but I definitely didn't expect Dr.Gray to come in the room ten minutes later with a smile on her face. "Umm...Do you know what's wrong?" I asked nervously.

"I do."

"And that is?" I asked because why the heck isn't she saying anything.

"Congratulations, Ava...You're pregnant." she said and my mouth went completely dry. Oh God.

"P-pregnant?...But how? I'm on the pill." I'm trying not to panic here.

"Well, birth control is not a hundred percent accurate.That's why it's still always best to use protection. And also you were sick recently and had to take antibiotics which can interfere with your birth control or other medicines that you may be taking."

Jesus Christ...I can't believe it. How will I even tell Max? We have never talked about children. Heck, we have never talked about the future at all. This is crazy...I'm going to be a mom. I'm freaking terrified. A tiny part of me is happy because I love Max and I do want children, but a huge part of me is freaking out.

After I was done freaking out Dr.Gray explained everything to me like my appointments and a whole lot of other crap. I was supposed to go into the office afterwards but I headed home instead. There was no way that I was going to get any work done after that bomb.

My mind is so cloudy that I don't know what to do. What will my parents think? Yes I am grown but I came here less than a year ago to work and now look at me, pregnant. I have got to call Max. I need him right now.

I tried calling him but didn't get an answer. I am assuming that he is in a meeting so I sent him a text and asked him to come to my place as soon as possible. About forty-five minutes later he was walking through the door in a panic.

When he saw me physically okay you could see him visibly relax. "Sweetheart, what's wrong? Are you okay?" he asked me. By the time he had made it here I had it all planned out. I knew exactly what I was going to say to him but now my mind is blank.

I can't talk and I feel sick to my stomach. I'm worried about his reaction and I can feel the tears form in my eyes. "Angel, tell me what's wrong… Please." He said in a soft tone.

"We…umm…we're gonna have a baby." I mumbled with my head slightly down. After a few seconds of him not saying anything I forced myself to look at him. He was just staring at me with a stoic expression.

"What did you say?" he asked me with his eyebrows furrowed as if he was confused.

"I'm pregnant." I said as I looked into his eyes pleading with him not to panic, to be there for me, for us.

All hopes of that happening died when he started slowly shaking his head. He slowly stood up and backed away.

"Max." I tried reaching for him.

"No…No." he said in a hoarse whisper as he shook his head.

"Max, don't leave…We need to talk…Please." I said with tears in my eyes as he reached for the doorknob and opened the door.

"Max." I tried to stop him but he just left. "MAX…Get back here." I yelled after him but it was pointless. He was gone. I told him that we are having a baby and he walked away from me.

The pain that I felt in that moment was unbearable. I fell to the floor and cried my eyes out. I couldn't believe that he left. I could understand if he panicked a little but to just walk away.

For a while I waited. In my mind he would turn around and come back. I just figured that he panicked and he needed a moment, but that moment turned into hours. By the time the sun came up my sadness and hurt had stepped aside to allow room for anger.

I was pissed with him for walking away from me. So what if he is scared, so am I. I needed him to be there for me.

As I sat there and had time to think I became even more pissed. At that moment I didn't want to talk to him. He walked out on me when I needed him and I will not allow him to come over today and be all apologetic. A simple apology won't fix how he made me feel.

I decided that I needed a few days away from him so I packed me a bag and left my apartment. By the time he gets his head out of his behind I will be gone.

My first stop was the bank. I'm not an idiot. Max has a lot of connections. If I use my debit card or my phone he will know where to find me within minutes. So I took out some cash, a lot of it. I called my parents and then I turned off my phone.

CHAPTER 27

Max's POV

When I woke up I had to look around and think for a minute. I was laid out on a couch but I wasn't home. As I sat up and looked around again I realized that I am at Justin's house. "Fuck." I groaned as I sat up. What the fuck? My head is killing me.

"You ready to tell me what the fuck is going on now?" I look up to see Justin sitting in a chair across the room. Then all of a sudden everything from yesterday came rushing back to me. Ava telling me that she is pregnant, clearly in tears and looking scared.

When she told me that she was pregnant I panicked. My first thought was that this is deja vu and that I can't let it happen again. I walked away from her. I drove around town for a while before I ended up at a bar.

I had way too many drinks and when I left to go home I came here instead. I needed to talk to

Justin but I guess I passed out before then.

"Fuck. What the fuck is wrong with me? What was I thinking?" I mumbled. This is fucking Ava. How could I fucking walk out on her? God, I'm stupid. I have to go see her. I picked up my phone to call her and it went straight to voicemail. Either her phone is off or I'm blocked. Both options would be because I'm a bastard.

"Fuck. I have to go."

"Max, what the fuck? Is everything alright?" Justin asked me but I was too fucked up to tell him.

"I don't know. Ava. I...I just have to go." I said as I rushed to the door.

"I'm going with you." he said, no doubt looking at how distraught I was.

I called Ava several times on the way to her house but still it went straight to her voicemail. "Baby...Please...I'm sorry, angel." I couldn't manage to say anything else. My hope and prayer is that she talks to me when I get to her place.

When I arrive I park my car and rush upstairs. Instead of using my key I knocked first but I didn't get an answer so I walked in. "AVA." I yelled for her but there was no response. "Angel?" my voice came out in a husky whisper as I walked through her apartment hoping that she was in her room. She wasn't there.

There were hangers everywhere and things

pulled out of her dresser. No, Ava. I felt like the world was crashing down on me. She was gone. I tried calling her again but her phone was still turned off.

"Angel, please talk to me. I didn't mean it. I know that you're hurting but just come back to me…Please." I croaked.

"Max, what's going on?" Justin asked.

"I fucked up…real bad. I have to find her." I whispered as tears started running down my face.

"What happened?" he asked.

"She umm…she told me that she was pregnant and…I…I…" I couldn't bring myself to say how I had walked out on her but he got what I was trying to say.

"You panicked." I nodded my head.

"Yeah and I left why she cried and yelled for me." I whispered, feeling even more ashamed than I was before.

"I fucking told you that this would happen…I told you to deal with your shit or it would fuck you up in the long run. Time doesn't heal everything, Max…You never dealt with your shit. You put it away and now…now you hurt Ava."

"Find her, Justin…Check her account because she had to go somewhere…I can't lose her…I need her…I need my family." I can't believe how stupid I was. I hurt Ava and now she is running away from me.

We headed back to my house so that we could try to find her. On the way there I did everything to try to reach her. I called her, text her, hell I even fucking emailed her. I even called Cammy to see if she had heard from her but she hadn't.

I almost called her mom even though I would hate to after what I had done. Then I thought about it, her and my mom have become close. I am sure if she knew she would tell my mom and since my phone hasn't rung with a death threat from her I assume that she doesn't know a thing.

Justin got to work on trying to track down Ava but nothing was coming up because her phone was turned off. Fuck. I don't know what I'm going to do.

"Oh shit." he said suddenly.

"What?" I asked nervously.

"Umm…Does Ava usually take out large sums of money at one time?"

"What kind of large sum?" I asked as I swallowed the lump that had formed in my throat.

"$20,000."

"Fuck…No she doesn't…She probably plans on staying away from me until she is ready to face me and she probably knew that I would track her card.

Fuck." I didn't know what the fuck to do. I know that I hurt her but I'm fucking devastated that she would stay away from me.

I hoped that she would change her mind and call me but she didn't. For hours I waited but she still didn't contact me or respond to anything.

"Max, just give her a little time. You know as well as anyone that you can't measure a person's hurt. Just give her some time. She will come back."

For days we did this same song and dance. I panicked and he tried talking me off of a ledge. Ava had covered all of her bases including emailing HR that she would be taking a leave. I just needed to know that she was okay so I took a different approach.

I emailed her not to say that I am sorry and to make it about us being together. I emailed her and simply asked her to just let me know that she was okay. I needed to know that she was okay and that her and the baby, our baby, were doing fine.

It was a little while later but she eventually emailed me back with a simple message, 'I'm fine'. I wanted to say so much more but for now that would have to do. I simply waited but when the week turned into weeks I started to lose my fucking mind.

By the end of the third week I was ready to do anything to bring her back. I didn't care what I had to do. I tried to think of anyone that she could be staying with but I couldn't.

Justin and I were just about to head to a meeting when a thought came to me. "Justin, what was the name of Ava's first helper?" I asked him.

"Tyler."

"Hmm...Call him in here...And Cammy too. I asked her before but things could have changed."

About five minutes later both of them came into my office. "Sir, you wanted to see me?" Tyler said.

"Yeah. Yeah I do." I said as I stepped from around my desk.

"Cammy, I have asked you this before but things could have changed...Have you heard anything from Ava?" I said a little more rough than I normally would but I was desperate.

"No, I haven't. I promise that I wouldn't lie to you about that." she said and I could tell that she wasn't lying so I looked to Tyler.

"And you? Have you heard from Ava at any point within the last three weeks?"

He hesitated. He fucking hesitated and I knew that he had. "No, Mr.Knight. I haven't heard from her, Sir." he said and I fucking snapped. The next second I had him pinned to the wall with my hand around his neck. How dare he hide her from me?

"Where the fuck is she? Tell me where she is right fucking now." I yelled. I blanked out. All I could see was red and if he didn't answer me we would have a big fucking problem.

"Max, let him go....Let him go." Justin said as he tried to pull me off.

"Please…Please don't hurt him." Cammy cried as she tried to get in between us to protect him. "Please don't hurt Tyler, Max."

I paused and took a deep breath, realizing how bad I had lost it. I dropped my hands and stepped back away from him. I shook my head and looked down, ashamed at how I had lost control.

"Look…I appreciate you looking out for Ava, but I need to know where she is and I need to know now."

CHAPTER 28

Ava's POV

The days away from Max have been torturous but I needed it. Our relationship went from nothing to a whole lot very fast. When I first left I did so because I was pissed. But I stayed away because I thought that maybe we needed a break, maybe we just happened too fast and adding a baby to the mix was just the straw that was too much.

Truthfully I miss Max so much, I really do. I just don't know how to deal with the hurt from him walking away from me. I needed him and it was just so easy for him to walk away without even speaking to me.

I have stayed in this hotel room for weeks now. He has tried to get me to come home but I wasn't ready. Now though I am not sure what hurts more, his reaction or being away from him.

I finally called my phone to check my voicemail that was full of messages from him. My heart broke with every message. Every time I heard his voice break as he pleaded with me to come home I could do nothing but cry.

I cried until I was too tired to do anything but close my eyes and sleep. At that moment I wanted nothing more than to be in his arms but I needed to rest first, I was exhausted and wasn't feeling well.

When I opened my eyes I thought that I was somehow still asleep and dreaming. Max was there. He was kneeling on the side of the bed while he held my hand and rubbed my stomach.

"Max…How are you here?" I asked him as tears started to fall down my cheeks.

"Shh…Don't cry, angel….Please don't cry." he said as he wiped my tears. "I'm so sorry, baby. I'm really sorry…Please come home…Come back to me. I promise that I will never hurt you again."

We needed to talk because there was so much that needed to be said. He needed to explain himself before anything but I couldn't stay away from him any longer. The relief that I felt in my heart when I saw him was like someone had lifted a huge boulder from my heart. Just having that feeling made me want to go home even if things are still rocky right now.

"Will you come home with me? I miss you so much and I'm so sorry for hurting you." he said with tears in his eyes.

"Okay." I mumbled.

He looked relieved that I agreed to go home with him. He pulled me in his arms and held me tight to his chest. I felt like I was home for the first time in weeks. I have missed him so much.

Once I was up and ready we left to head to his house. We rode home in complete silence. Max held me close and didn't let me go the whole time while Jensen drove us. When I walked into the living room I realized just how much I had missed him and being here.

I know that it was my choice to leave but maybe I shouldn't have stayed away for so long. "Don't cry, baby." Max said as he pulled me into his arms.

I didn't even realize that I was crying but at that moment I broke down completely. I sobbed in his chest while he lifted me and carried me to the bedroom.

He laid us down and he held me while I cried. When I had finally calmed down he leaned back a little and looked into my eyes. "I missed you so much...You left me." he said in a soft voice as he frowned.

"You left me first." I mumbled and he looked ashamed before looking down and away from me.

"Why, Max?...Why did you do that?" He stared

at me for a moment without saying a word. I got out of bed to leave. If he didn't want to talk then fine.

"Ava...Please stay." he said with tears in his eyes.

"No, Max...You never want to talk about your past and I let you be. I decided that I would leave it alone until you were ready but not anymore. Now it has affected me. You left me, Max, while I was scared out of my mind about the baby and the only thing that I wanted was for you to tell me that everything would be okay and that you would be there. So, no. Either you start talking or I am leaving and going to my apartment."

"Okay...Okay...I will talk but please, Ava... Please don't leave again...I can't take it." he pleaded with me.

"Talk." I said firmly as I sat on the bed.

"I..umm...I was engaged before...A few years ago I was engaged. I had loved that girl since I was in high school. We finally got together in college and I thought that she just finally saw me but I was wrong...I proposed to her and she accepted but a few days before the wedding she disappeared."

When he spoke he didn't seem as though he was still hurt by it but then he paused and I could see the hurt in his eyes. I knew then that there was more that he needed to say.

"I saw her some months later and she was pregnant with what I thought was my child. She told me that it was my child but that she didn't want me to be involved...I..I begged her...She let me fucking beg her to be in a child's life that she knew wasn't mine...I didn't find out until I got a blood test done when the baby was born."

I could tell that he was fighting back tears. I can't imagine how hurt he must have been. I wrapped my arms around him, wanting to take his pain away. "Max, I would never do anything like that to you. I wouldn't do that to anyone." I said to him.

"I know...I really do know that, angel. I just kind of lost it at that moment but I know better, trust me I do. I am so fucking sorry for putting you through that. I never want to go through that again. I have dealt with a lot of hurt behind losing that child but no pain was greater than the feeling that I had when I thought that you weren't going to come back to me...I'm sorry, baby." he said as he looked into my eyes.

I knew that he was. The reaction that he had was hurtful but I know that Max would never intentionally hurt me. I want us to be together and be a family. I want to focus on us and our future so I made the choice to put it behind us.

"I forgive you."

He held me tighter while we both cried in each

other's arms. I love him so much and that hasn't changed and I am sure that it never will. "I love you, Ava." he said as he kissed me for the first time since we have been back together.

"I love you too. But , Max…I want you to get a dna test when the baby is born." I hated that his past caused him to be uncertain about us and I don't want that hanging over us at any time.

"What? Why? I don't need one."

"I don't want there to be any doubt. You were my first. You're the only man that has touched me so I know that the baby is yours. I want you to be sure about it too."

Is the whole thing hurtful? Yes. But considering what he has been through I wouldn't be mad at all if he needed a dna test.

"Angel, I'm sorry for ever making you feel this way but I want you to know that I have no doubt. I know that the baby is mine just like you're mine."

CHAPTER 29

Max's POV

I was very close to losing the best thing that has ever happened to me all because of something in my past. Justin was right those few years ago when he kept telling me that I needed to deal with my hurt. I just kept moving forward because I didn't want to deal with how much it had actually hurted me.

I admit I was devastated. I really loved that child and even though it hurted for her not to be mine, it hurt even more for me to have to leave her with her mom. I didn't think that Audrey would ever change, not even for her own kid. At the time I wished that I could have just kept the baby but I had no rights to her. She wasn't mine.

Now though I have an opportunity to be a father and I plan to be the best father that my little baby could ever have. I feel like shit for walking out on Ava. I can't imagine how hurt she feels and I know that I have to make it up to her but I'm just so thankful that she is here.

"How long are you going to watch me sleep?" Ava said as she turned towards me and I smiled at her.

"I can't help it. I'm just happy that you're here. I missed you so much."

"Mhm…Well, if you miss me so much you should show me…make love to me, Max." she said before she leaned in and kissed me.

I took off my clothes before slowly undressing her as I kissed every inch of her body. I moved between her legs and slid inside of her as I moaned her name. It had been weeks since I felt the warmth of her pussy and it felt so fucking good.

I made love to her slowly. I wanted to pour out my love to her and my feelings. I wanted her to feel how sorry I was for hurting her and how much I love her.

I moved in and out of her slowly but hard. Her body started to tremble and I knew that she was about to cum. "M-Max." she moaned as she came hard. As she came she slowly opened her eyes and looked into mine as tears slid down her cheeks.

I kissed her tears away before kissing her on her sweet lips. "I love you, angel. I love you so much." I said to her as I emptied my cum inside her.

Having sex with Ava is always amazing.

Fucking her is out of this world good, but making love to her after being away from her for three weeks, is something that I will never forget. I never want to be away from her again.

After we had both came down from the feelings of our love making we laid in each other's arms until Ava was hungry. We had dinner delivered because neither one of us wanted to leave. While we ate we talked about everything that happened between us. The conversation was going good until she asked me a dreaded question.

"So, you never answered my question earlier. How did you find me?" she asked me. There was no need to lie to her. I'm sure with office gossip that she would find out anyway.

"Tyler told me where you were." I said and was hoping to leave it at that but I had no such luck.

"Willingly? Because I know you when it comes to me." she asked me as she narrowed her eyes.

"I wouldn't say willingly, no. He tried to say that he didn't know where you were and I knew that he was lying."

"And you did what after that?" Jesus, will she just let it go.

"Ava."

"Max." And there goes her stubbornness. She wasn't going to let this go so it is what it is.

"I kind of lost my shit. I snapped…And would do it again as long as I got you back." I said firmly and I fucking meant it. I don't give a shit who I have to snap on.

"You owe him an apology, Max. He was just helping me. I had no one else to help me so you need to apologize…Did you tell your mom about the baby?" she asked and I had to laugh. She must think that I am stupid.

"Fuck no. I didn't tell her."

"Why?" She had the nerve to look confused.

"So she can kill me for running you off. No thanks. I'm not an idiot." She laughed at that because she knows how my mom can be.

Ava's POV

I was happy to be home with Max. Ever since he has seen me he has barely given my stomach space. I have a small bump and he just keeps rubbing it. I'm only three months and I have a long way to go which was a part of our conversation.

Max didn't want me to work anymore. He wanted me to stay home which is ridiculous. I won't even be staying home after the baby is born. He didn't like it but he will get over it. I don't care how much money he has, I love my job so until that changes I will continue to work.

A few days later after I had returned we finally went into the office. It was a little awkward at first. I mean I did disappear a few weeks ago and came back like nothing happened. Not to mention that I have this small baby bump that is slightly noticeable if you are close to me.

The day went about as good as it could. We also sat down and had a conversation with Tyler. I really appreciated him for helping me and he didn't deserve to be on the receiving end of Max's anger.

I'm surprised that he didn't quit or sue Max but he assured us that he wasn't going to and we are glad. Tyler is a great asset to the company and we would hate to lose him. He is also a great friend.

I'm currently getting ready for my girls' luncheon. I don't hang with a lot of people here but it's always fun with Cammy and Lindsey. They are both lively and fun without a filter.

"Ava. Ava." Cammy says as she comes through the door. Of course she would arrive first because Lindsey is always late even when she is hosting.

"Hey, Cammy…Can't wait for the girl's chat. It's been a while."

"Mhm. And thanks to your crazy man I have something sort of good to tell." she says with excitement.

"Mmm…Me too and I can not wait. Lindsey needs to hurry her behind up."

"I'm here, jeez. Everyone knows that I am always late so there is no use in complaining anymore." she shrugged and we all laughed because she is absolutely correct.

"Okay, girls. Bring on the wine. We have lots to talk about." Lindsey says as she wiggles her eyebrows. "Soo…who wants to go first?"

"I guess I should so that you won't waste a good glass of wine on me…I'm pregnant." I squeal.

"Oh my God." They screamed in unison and hugged me.

"This is so fucking exciting. I'm going to be an auntie. I can't wait. How did Max take it?" she asked with a wince.

"Umm…Well…"

"Oh no. What happened?" Cammy asked.

"Lindsey, you can't repeat anything that happens during girl chat, remember?" I said and she nodded her head and looked concerned. "I just don't want you to tell your mom. He definitely doesn't want her to know because she will be upset with him."

"Okay. I promise not to say anything."

"He…He kind of freaked out when I told him. He…umm…He just left."

"What do you mean by he left?" Lindsey asked.

"I mean he left. He didn't even say anything. He turned around and left." I shrugged. I personally don't like talking about this but this is what we do when we get together. We share our personal lives.

"Oh God, Ava. Is that why you left?" Cammy asked and I nodded my head.

"I was so hurt and I just needed some time away from him but you know how he is. He wouldn't have allowed me the space to think so I left."

I wasn't sure how Lindsey would feel because he is her brother but surprisingly she didn't judge. She understood Max but she also understood my need to leave him for that moment.

"Well, thanks to your little disappearing act Tyler and I have actually communicated a little." Cammy said and I was shocked. He has been hell bent on not giving anyone a chance even though I can tell that he likes Cammy too.

"I know you know what happened because of us all talking in the office but yeah we talked after that. I honestly was terrified that Max was going to hurt him and couldn't control my emotions. I hated being so vulnerable in front of him but we are at least getting to know each other now." she said with a smile.

"I'm so happy for you, Cammy. I hope that everything works out for you with Tyler." I said and I really do.

Cammy deserves happiness. Tyler does too but he is a closed book. He is a great friend when it comes to being there for someone but when it comes to his life he isn't a big sharer.

"Well, girls...Things have been going really good with me and Justin. Cammy, I don't think that you know but we moved in together. We didn't want to wait." Lindsey said.

"I don't blame you. I wouldn't have wanted to wait either. I mean the whole situation was fucked up but seriously I wouldn't have wanted to leave for one second after that." Cammy said and I agreed.

What they went through was hard and I couldn't imagine having to stay away from Max like that but at the same time have to constantly see him.

Lindsey goes to the kitchen and comes back with a wine glass. "Here you go, pregnant lady."

"And what's this?" I asked because I am being very cautious.

"Apple juice. I wouldn't dare give you alcohol. I'm the best Tee Tee in the world." she smirks.

"Okay...Let's make a toast." Lindsey said.

"Here's to the months ahead of us. It may have taken each of us a while or some trouble to get here but we are here now. We are going to enjoy the ride. Cheers, ladies."

CHAPTER 30

Max's POV (months later)

Life has been fucking great. Ava's pregnancy has flown by. I can't believe that we will be welcoming our little one soon. We have no idea what we are having. I of course wanted to know but she let our mothers talk her into waiting.

Those two have gotten on my last fucking nerves from the moment that they knew that they would be grandmothers. It's always Max you need to do this and you need to do that. Buy this before the baby comes and Ava wants this but hasn't said anything.

It's just been a big fucking headache. Hell we even moved out of the penthouse and bought a home. Our mothers insisted that their grandchild has a yard and plenty of space to move around. Considering that the baby hasn't popped out of Ava's pussy yet I don't see why that couldn't wait.

Much to my displeasure they took Ava to look at houses and of course she fell in love with one and what Ava wants she gets. So a few months ago we moved into this ridiculous size house that she claims will be our forever home.

Yeah right. As soon as them old ladies get her to looking again I will be buying something else. I will give her whatever she wants though as long as she stays with me.

We have since worked out all of our bullshit from when she left me. It took a while but we are so much better after what we went through.

Our only problem has been her ass not wanting to be home. She is determined to work until she pops. So her office was moved closer to mine and the office in between ours was turned into her resting room.

She didn't like that very much but who gives a shit. That's a compromise because I want to fire her ass but that won't go well at all. And as stubborn as she has become she will probably go out and find another job just to spite me.

Ring Ring- Looking down at my phone I see that it's none other than my mother. What could she possibly want now?

Me: Yes

Mom: That's no way to answer your phone. What's your problem?

Me: Just wondering what you and Linda want me to do now.

Mom: Wow. I can't call my only son just to check on him.

Me: Sure you can but that's not why you're calling. Ever since you found out that Ava was pregnant none of your calls are to check on me. What do you need, mom?

Mom: Well, since you're going to force me I guess we need to discuss the baby shower.

Sure I forced her. Bullshit. That's why she was calling anyway.

Me: There isn't a baby shower because Ava doesn't want one. She is also due in two weeks so she isn't about to stress over one either.

Mom: Well, me and Linda were talking and we decided that we wanted a shower. It's our first grandbaby, Max. So we planned it and it's going to be this Saturday. Have fun telling Ava. Bye.

With that she hangs up. She knew what the fuck she was doing. Of course she didn't want to tell Ava. Pregnant Ava is not my angel Ava. She is fucking moody. She is a whole brat and if she doesn't get her way she gets angry, really angry.

I love her carrying my baby but fuck I can't wait to have my angel back. Now she has said for the past almost six months that she did not want a damn shower and here they go planning one anyway and leaving it to me to tell her.

Speaking of Ava here she comes walking through the door, locking it, and closing the blinds. "Hey, babe." She says all sweet even though there was nothing sweet about her this morning when she had pancakes instead of waffles.

"Hey, angel...How are you feeling?" I eyed her suspiciously because at this point you can never tell what she is up to.

"Horny." she said as she slid my papers away and sat on my desk in front of me. I swear I feel like I'm being used for my dick with these pregnancy hormones.

I stood up and slid my hand under her dress to rub her pussy. "Fuck...You're fucking soaked." I groaned. I dropped my pants and slid right into her.

"Mmm." she moaned. I fucked her slowly because I needed to make her beg.

"H-harder, Max. I want it harder." she moaned.

"If I fuck you harder you have to do something for me. Will you do it?"

"Y-yes." she moaned.

"You'll do anything for me, baby, hmm?"

"Yes…anything." she moaned.

"Promise me."

"I promise…Please, Max." she cried out as I hit her spot. I put her out of her miserably and fucked her harder and faster until she was coming so hard that she couldn't even speak. She just laid on the desk while she trembled.

"Fuck." I groaned as I released into her.

Coming down from our orgasms I winced because I know that she is about to have a fit. "My mom and your mom planned a baby shower for you this weekend. I didn't know." I said to her and before I could brace myself she smacked me in the chest.

"Ow…What the hell?" I yelled.

"You tricked me and you know it." she groaned.

"I'm sorry, baby, but the mothers tricked me first. Just let them have this one thing so I won't have to hear it. Please." Shit I'm not too proud to beg. As long as I don't have to put up with her, my mama, or my mother in law's bullshit I will do it.

I have to keep all three of them happy in order to live in peace. My father and father in law do not help at all. They think that the shit is funny.

"Fine. I will go, sex slave." she smirked.

"I told you about calling me that...After my baby comes out I'm going to show you what a sex slave is." I smack her on her ass as she got up.

I killed two birds with one stone. I made the grandmothers happy and made Ava cum. Now I can get back to my busy as fuck work day. There is a lot of shit that I need to get done before Ava pops because I won't be leaving her or my kid for a while.

It won't be much longer before my little one gets here. Ava has no idea but as soon as she gives birth I'm going to ask her to marry me. I honestly have wanted to for a long time but I didn't want her to think that I was only asking her because she got pregnant.

We have had quite a few battles with her thinking that I was only staying with her because of the baby. I hated that I put that insecurity in her. I never wanted that. I just had to work through my own bullshit.

I finish working and get my shit ready so that I can grab Ava's sleeping ass and leave. I swear she didn't like that damn resting room but she damn sure be knocked the fuck out in there.

"I'm going to use the bathroom. I will meet you at the elevator?" Ava said and I nodded my head before heading out. I was almost out of the door when Justin's ass came waltzing in.

"What do you want?" I groan.

"Don't be like that. I mean she thought that she locked the door." he smirked.

Him and Lindsey really make me sick. I walked into his office earlier to her spreaded out over his fucking desk. Thankfully she wasn't naked but you couldn't miss his head under her fucking dress.

"No fucking at the job. It's unethical."

"Says the man who had to pause a meeting because Ava needed some. Yeah okay." He is such an asshole.

"Yeah well no fucking my sister in this building then..Ugh...I can't stand y'all." I groan with disgust. They can't keep their fucking hands off of each other. I mean I'm happy for them but damn lets not forget that it's my best friend and my little sister.

"Anyway, I came in here to tell you that everything is set up for when Ava pops. I'm sure it won't be long because the girl is freaking huge." he said and I smirk because he has no idea that Ava is behind him.

"What are you smirking at?" he asked and before I could respond she whacked him across the head.

"A-Ava...I...umm." he stutters and it's hilarious.

"Yeah, yeah. I know that I'm freaking huge. Look at Max. Of course he would impregnate me with a giant of a kid." Now how did this turn into her talking about me.

"Come on, baby. Let's go so that we can eat." When in the hot seat always feed the pregnant woman.

When we finally left the office we went out to dinner before heading home to relax. The best part of my day is being home with my baby. There is nothing better.

After dealing with so much bullshit I never would have guessed that my life would be as good as it is now. Ava came into my life and erased every piece of hurt and pain that I ever felt. Nothing could ever compare to just being with her.

CHAPTER 31

Ava's POV

Ugh. I'm so tired of carrying this baby. Max thinks that my baby bump is the cutest thing ever but it's freaking tiring. My stomach is huge. At one point I thought that I was carrying twins but thankfully it's just one.

I am currently laying here trying to pretend to be still sleeping. I don't want to get up and get the day started. It's the day of this stupid baby shower that I did not want at all.

I really didn't see a point in having one. Anything that I even contemplated on buying Max had it sent to the house. So the baby doesn't need anything and I don't care for the attention but my mama and his mama took it upon themselves to give me one. They say that we were robbing them of their grandmotherly rights. Whatever.

"Angel…It's time to get up, baby." Max whispers in my ear.

"Why do I have to get up when you tricked me into going today?"

"I'm sorry, baby. I will make it up to you." he said before kissing me.

I may as well get up because I can't get out of this day. I know that if I don't go I would be in trouble with the grandmothers. When I walk out to the living room I am surprised to see a big breakfast spread out on the table.

I looked at Max and he had the biggest smile on his face. "I wanted you to relax a bit before we get going. Have a good breakfast and just sit back and relax." His smile is so cute.

He is the absolute sweetest. I owe him so much once I have this baby. I have been a lot with my crazy hormones. He is always so understanding and just tells me that it's okay but it's not. He has been so perfect through it all.

While we ate I just couldn't stop thinking about how great my life is right now. I can't believe that I am in New York, I have Max, and I am about to be a mom.

"I love you, Max. You make me feel like the luckiest woman in the world." I lean in to kiss him. Feeling his lips on mine always does unexplainable things to me. I wish that we could stay home the whole day and get lost in each other.

"As much as I love this, baby, we have to get

moving." Max interrupted my beautiful thoughts.

When we finally walked into my baby shower a couple of hours later I was brought to tears at how beautiful everything was. We don't know what we're having so they did the whole thing in blue, pink, and gold. The colors were so beautiful together.

"Aww. Don't cry, Ava." my mom said as she hugged me.

"Everything is so beautiful. I didn't want to come but I'm happy that I did." I said as I wiped my tears.

Everything turned out perfectly. The shower was unisex so it was a lot of fun seeing the guys play games. We laughed really hard when Max, Justin, and Tyler teamed up for a game. They had to deliver a baby.

Justin was the pregnant woman, Max was the dad, and Tyler was the doctor. It was super hilarious. I have to say that by the end of the shower I was extremely happy to have had one. I just looked at it as our last free moment to enjoy our friends.

By the end of the evening I was exhausted and happy to be back at home and laying in Max's arms. We relaxed and watched movies until late in the night when I was ready for Max to make love to me.

Like every night Max slid into me, filling

me up completely. I had gotten so big and uncomfortable that we now had to have sex with him standing on the side of the bed. It still felt so good as he moved in and out of me at a slow and torturous pace.

"Max, you feel so good." I moaned. He started moving faster and I was so close. I was climbing fast and I knew that in a moment I was going to cum until I am all of a sudden soaked.

"What the fuck?" Max said as he jumped back. I was slightly confused for a split second until it came to me.

"Oh, God. My water broke." I yelled.

"Oh shit." Max said with wide eyes.

I wasn't sure if he was going to pass out or just stand there stuck. "Max...Snap out of it. Help me up so that we can go to the hospital." How am I the one going into labor and he is the one freaking out?

"Fuck. Sorry, baby. Let me grab us some clothes." he said as he headed to the closet.

We got dressed quickly and headed to the hospital. By the time that we made it there and they hooked me up to monitors I was six centimeters. I was shocked because I was barely in any pain.

"Fuck. I need to call our mothers." Max said.

"No...I just want it to be me and you for a while.

We can call them in the morning."

I know that it was selfish but oh well. My mom came to visit when I got later in my pregnancy and she won't be leaving until after my six weeks are up. Probably more like when the baby is a couple of months old. I tried convincing her that she would miss dad but since she has Max flying him in every couple of weeks that didn't work.

We are very close and I love all of them but I want this moment to just be with me and him. "If you are sure that is what you want then fine. Whatever makes you happy." he said before kissing me.

I was thankful that I wasn't in much pain when I arrived but as time went on the contractions became more painful. I was so thankful for Max because he was the best. He held my hand through it all and whispered sweet words to calm me down.

A few hours later I was pushing and it wasn't long before I heard the sweet cries of my baby. "Alright, dad. You want to tell mom what it is?" Dr.Gray asked. Max was beaming with his eyes full of tears as he looked down.

He could barely hold it together when he looked at me. "It's a boy...We have a baby boy, Angel." he said through his tears.

"We have a son." I sobbed when they laid him

on my chest. "I love you, baby boy." I whispered to him.

This was it. I knew that this moment would change my life forever. I was now a mom to a baby boy. He had the sweetest little cry and he looked every bit of Max.

They took him to clean him up before bringing him back so that I could feed him. I was in heaven. It was nothing like giving birth to him and laying there feeding my boy for the first time.

"So, daddy, what did you decide to name him?" I asked him. He smiled as he took the baby from my arms.

"Let's see, my big man...How about Noah Alexander?"

"Sounds perfect. Noah Alexander Knight. I love it." I said with a huge smile on my face.

He held Noah as he spoke to him. It was so sweet and then he shocked me. "Noah, I promise to love you and your mother always. I promise to take care of your mother. I promise that I will never make her cry again, not as your mother, not as my woman, and definitely not as my wife." I was speechless.

"W-what?" I asked eventually with wide eyes. He placed Noah back into my arms and I watched him as he got down on one knee. I instantly started to cry.

"Ava, I have wanted to ask you this for a long time but I wanted to wait until this moment when I can look you and our baby in the eyes and promise you my love forever. I thought that I knew love before but I didn't, not until I met you. And now being here with you and Noah is the greatest feeling in the world. I want this forever and I promise to love you with my whole heart for the rest of my days. I love you, Angel. Will you marry me?"

I couldn't speak. I couldn't do anything but cry so I just nodded my head. He slipped the most beautiful ring on my finger and I cried harder. "I love you too." I said in between sobs.

Max leaned in and kissed my tears before he climbed onto the bed with me and Noah. I was overfilled with joy. Here I am lying here with my family, my baby boy and my fiance. I wouldn't want to be anywhere else in this world.

"Are you ready to feel the wrath of our mothers?"

"Yeah but I'm putting all of the blame on you." I laughed but in all seriousness I would take it because it was worth it.

Max Facetimed both of them in a group and when they answered they immediately started squealing with excitement.

"Oh my God...He is so beautiful...Why didn't

you call us to come?" my mom said with tears in her eyes.

Before we could respond both mothers started fussing at Max, assuming that he was the one that didn't want them to come. It's a logical assumption because they have been working on his last nerves and he hasn't kept quiet about it at all.

I could tell that he was getting frustrated so I wanted to shut them up. I slowly lifted my hand and rested it on Max's arm that he was holding Noah in and they once again screamed.

"You proposed?" his mom asked and he nodded.

They were in heaven after that and all was forgiven. We ended the call knowing that they would be coming soon. We laid back and enjoyed being there with just our little family for now.

CHAPTER 32

Max's POV

On the first night that we were at home with Noah I was in heaven. I mean sure he woke up through the night and it took a lot of energy but I loved it. Although Ava breastfed him I didn't want to miss a thing so I woke up with her every time.

I wanted to make sure that she knew that I would be there with her through it all so everything that I could do I did. I changed him. I bathe him and put him to sleep. She had a big enough job just feeding him because the kid eats like his daddy.

True to my word I have done that every single day and night so today will be difficult for me. After two months of being home with my family I am heading into the office to get some meetings done. Ava insisted that I get back to doing meetings since we had some pending deals that were left incomplete when she went into labor.

Walking into the office was hard when I

wanted to be home with them but I knew that she was right. "Morning, stranger." Justin said as he came into my office.

"How am I a stranger when you just saw me?" I looked at him like he had gone crazy. "You saw me when I came to see my Godson, not at work."

"Yeah yeah. Let's get started."

We went through our usual Monday morning routine before heading into a meeting with our board. A meeting that I am sure to be long as shit since I have been off for a whole two months.

"Alright, Ladies and Gentlemen. Let's get started." I said as I entered the room. The room was dead silent. "You all wanted this meeting, not me. So if you have anything that you need to say then say it because I could have been at home with my family."

"Sir, we don't mean to be disrespectful but we wanted to just touch base with you. You haven't been to work in two months nor have you done much work from home. You already had pending deals that needed tending to. We just wanted to check on things." one of them says.

I smirked and tried to remember that it's normal for them to want to be in the know. "In the months that I have been away have you lost any money? Matter of fact I can guarantee that your bank account has increased. So you tell me how you not actually losing money is more important than the birth of my son." I said firmly.

Again I receive silence. "Let me explain something to you, you are here because you were a part of the business before it belonged to me but make no mistake, I don't need you. I made decisions to bring this company from where it was to a billion dollar company. So if you feel that I'm not working up to your standards you're welcome to leave but my family will always come first." I said it and I fucking meant it.

Before I could continue, my phone started to vibrate and my watch showed me that it was Ava. She knew that I was in a meeting so her calling alarmed me a little. I knew that I needed to finish this meeting so I asked Justin to see what she needed or if something was going on and she needed me to leave.

I got back started on my meeting and was almost done with them when Justin came back in. The look on his face made me pause because I knew that something was wrong.

Ava's POV

My morning started off great. I woke up with Noah and then me and him said our goodbyes to Max as he went into work. The rest of the morning was spent relaxing and talking with my mom about the wedding. Since it was Max's first day back at the office she came over to spend the day with me.

The doorbell rang and I was surprised since I wasn't expecting anyone. When I opened the door I was even more surprised to see one of the workers from our old apartment building. "Hey, Paul. Is something wrong?" I asked.

"I'm sorry to bother you, Miss Ava, but a package was delivered to the old building for Mr.Knight. It had no return address but the delivery person said that it was time sensitive. I tried calling Mr.Knight's office but couldn't get him so I checked you all's forwarding address."

"Oh. Okay. Well, thank you for that." I said as I moved to get the package.

"It's a little heavy, ma'am. I can bring it in for you."

"Thank you, Paul."

He brought in the package. I tipped him and then he left. I was curious about the package because Max wouldn't have ordered anything and forgot to change the address so I decided to open it.

When I did I almost passed out. "Mom…What the hell? Come here. Grab Noah." I said in a panic. Inside of this huge box was a small kid balled up. I lifted her out and checked her. She didn't move a muscle but she was breathing.

"Oh God. Whose child is that?" my mother asked. Who the hell puts a baby in a box? She was small but you can tell that she must be at least four or five years old. She was dirty and looked very much neglected.

"Ava, there is a note in the box." my mom said. I grabbed the note and read it. My stomach was in knots. Whoever stuffed this poor child in this box claimed that this little girl belonged to Max and that she was his responsibility now.

I tried to call him but he didn't answer. I knew that he had meetings this morning but this couldn't wait. A few minutes later I got a call from Justin.

Me: Hello.

Justin: Hey, Ava. Max is in a meeting. He told me to call and see if everything is okay.

Me: No everything isn't okay. You tell Maximo to get his ass the fuck home before I fucking kill him right now.

I hung up after that. I was furious at all of this. I didn't know whether to call the police or what so I waited for Max. The child was so dirty though so I wet some towels so that I could clean her off and

I called Jensen to bring me some clothes and other things for her. This whole situation is a mess, a fucking mess.

"Ava, you need to calm down. You don't know what's going on but listen to Max before you lose your emotions." my mom said. It felt like forever before he finally made it through the door.

CHAPTER 33

Max's POV

When Justin told me what Ava said on the phone I immediately ended the meeting. Ava doesn't even fucking curse so I knew that something crazy was going on but I definitely didn't expect what I came home to.

When I walked through the door she was sitting on the couch holding a little girl with some dirty and torn clothes. She was feeding her some kind of sandwich. I was so confused, so fucking confused.

"Angel, what's going on?" I asked as I slowly walked into the living room. Hell the look on her face had me scared for my damn life. She looked like she wanted to kill me.

She stood up with the little girl and handed me a letter. The letter was utter bullshit and I knew that it could only come from one person. I'm not sure why after all of this time that she would still be trying to fuck up my life but I wasn't about to let her.

"I can't fucking believe this shit. You fucking…"

"First of all, watch your mouth. You don't even curse like that and you're in front of Noah and this little girl. Now I'm trying to be patient because I understand how this looks but calm down." she huffed and crossed her arms.

She was trying to be tough but I know her. I can see the tears in her eyes and know that she is about to lose it. I wasn't about to do this in front of Noah though so I asked her mother to watch both of them so that we could talk.

"Come here." I said to Ava.

"No." she huffed. There goes that stubborn shit again but the problem is today I'm not dealing with it. I don't have the energy to.

"Ava. Now." I said to her firmly through gritted teeth.

When we walked into our bedroom I had to take a moment before I could talk to her. I was hurt by her believing anything like this. She knows that she can talk to me instead of acting like this.

"Ava, you know better than what you're thinking right now."

"How?" was her only response. I took a deep breath to keep from losing my shit.

"First of all, I would hope that you would know me enough to know that I would never keep me having a child away from you. You sat there while I explained how hurt I was when I thought a child was mine but she wasn't. Do you really think that I would have a child and not be in her life, hmm? I also would never allow my child to be in the condition that the child was in. If you think that I would be that negligent do you also think that I will neglect you and Noah?" I asked her because I wanted to know.

She didn't say anything. "Answer me, Ava. Do you think that I would neglect my fucking child, hmm?"

I was starting to get pissed off. Now was not the time for her to be on her stubborn shit. I needed her to look me in my face and tell me that she knew better than this shit.

"No. I don't think that...Max, I...I'm sorry. I wasn't thinking." she mumbled.

"No you weren't. Now get yourself together so that we can figure this shit out." I shook my head at the bullshit that has once again come into my life. She just nodded her head before grabbing my hand.

"Are you mad?" Hell yeah I was fucking mad but she has been going through her own shit too and I wasn't about to hurt her feelings.

"No, baby. I just want to get to the bottom of this because I'm sure that this has something to do with my ex. I just need to call Justin real quick." I wanted to be honest with her about the situation. I'm not keeping any of it away from her. I gave Justin a call because I need his help.

Justin: Fuck. I'm glad to hear from you. Ava sounded scary. I thought that she was going to kill you for sure.

Me: I'm sure that she wanted to. I need you to come to the house and make sure that you bring your laptop.

Justin: Shit. Is everything alright?

Me: Fuck no. I think that crazy bitch left her baby on my fucking door step in a fucking box.

Justin: What the fuck? I'm on the way.

For the life of me I can't figure out what I may have done for Audrey to want to obviously torture me my whole life. The bitch has to be insane. It's like a continuous cycle of just being an evil bitch but this time she has gone too damn far.

When I walked back to the living room Jensen was bringing in bags and bags of shit. "What's all of this?" I asked.

"I...She needed some things. I asked Jensen to

get them." Ava said with a guilty look on her face because a few things I don't mind but it's bags and bags of shit.

"Ava." I said to her as a warning. She nodded her head.

"I just...She needs a bath. Take Noah so that I can clean her up."

"Come here, buddy." I said as I took my son into my arms. "What am I going to do with your mother?" I asked him as if he would know. I already know how this shit is about to happen because I can see it in her eyes. This little girl not being mine doesn't mean a thing. Ava is going to want to keep her regardless.

A little while later Justin came walking through the door. "Man, what the fuck is going on? Did that crazy bitch really do that?" he asked.

"I'm assuming that it's her. I mean I don't know anyone else that it could be."

"What do you mean you assume?"

"Well, between having to get Ava's ass together, her buying this shit, and now she is in there bathing the little girl I haven't had a chance to dig into it." I rubbed my face trying to relax a little.

"Fuck." he said, probably thinking the same thing as me. Ava isn't going to just let this shit go. "Okay. Well, you go take care of that and I will start digging."

Thankfully Noah had fallen asleep so I took him to the nursery before going to find Ava. When I found her she was in one of the guest rooms and had just finished dressing the little girl. I sat down on the bed and took a deep breath. This is a little child. No matter what I have to remember to stay calm.

"Sweetheart, what's your name?" I asked her.

"Aurora." she mumbled in a soft voice.

"What is your mom and dad's name?"

"Daddy's name is Maximo Knight and I don't have a mommy."

What the fuck? I'm so fucking confused right now. "Who did you live with, sweetheart?" I asked because what does she mean she doesn't have a mommy.

"My nanny Audrey. Her said that daddy needed me to stay with her for a while." I'm floored. What the fuck kind of game is she playing? She would do this to her own kid.

The last time that we talked she made it seem as though she took care of her kid but obviously not. The child doesn't even know that she was her mother.

"And where is Audrey now?" I asked her. Panic and fear was in her eyes as she started to cry.

"The man hurt her." Aurora mumbled.

"What do you mean, sweetheart?"

"He...he was so mad. He was yelling."

"What did he say?"

"Can I say a bad word?" She looked up to me as she spoke.

"Yes this time." I said.

"The money. Where is the fucking money? She didn't tell him. Then he got mad and pushed her. Her hit her head and her was bleeding." She said as she started to cry.

"Max, give her a break. She needs a break." Ava said as she hugged Aurora. I felt bad for this little girl not only because of her fucked up mother but also because of what she had to witness.

I stepped out of the room so that I could talk to Justin. He was doing some digging on Audrey. "Find anything?" I asked him because I knew that it wouldn't take him long. If Justin wasn't so loyal to me he could have a good career doing investigative work.

"I found a whole fucking lot. Audrey was involved in some heavy shit. She took her scamming up a notch...I don't know how in the hell we never knew this but her past is a mess. She even had been blackmailing a few men after sleeping with them. They would wake up after a night with her only to find their money and valuables missing. Then after stealing their shit she would still blackmail them for more. The bitch is fucking crazy."

"Yeah, well, she must have scammed the wrong fucking one this time because according to Aurora, that's the little girl's name by the way, a man came to Audrey asking about money and she said that he pushed her and she was bleeding."

"Fuck."

"Yeah. So see if you can find out where she was staying and send the police for a wellness check. I'm giving Aurora a break for a few minutes because she was upset. I need to know more before we contact someone to come get her. I want to know how she ended up on my fucking doorstep."

"Gotcha."

This is nothing but a fucking shit show. I headed back to the guest room. I'm not trying to be an asshole about the kid but I am desperate to get all of the answers that she can give.

When I walked back in the room Ava was holding Aurora but she had calmed down so I wanted to continue our talk. "Come here, sweetheart." I said as I opened my arms to Aurora. She hesitated to leave Ava but she came to me anyway.

I am instantly taken back to the moment that she was born. I still remember the moment that I heard her cry and how I felt. I have to swallow the lump that has formed in my throat from the memory.

"I just need to ask you a few more questions, okay." I said and she nodded her head. "How did you get here? Who brought you to my house if Audrey was hurt?"

"Umm. I don't know how I got here. Nanny Audrey's mommy came over. Her cried when her saw Nanny Audrey. Her gave me the gummies that Nanny Audrey gives me and when I woke up I was here." she shrugged.

Confused isn't the word that I am right now. I'm assuming whatever the fuck is in those fucking gummies makes her sleep. But from what Audrey has always said she doesn't talk to her fucking mother. Her mother was supposedly this horrible person but from what I have experienced the apple doesn't fall too far from the fucking tree.

"Ava, take her to your mother for a minute. We need to talk before Noah wakes up." I said and she nodded her head but I can tell that she wanted to protest. When she came back she slowly came into the room.

"I just wanted to give you a heads up that I was going to call the authorities now so they can get a report and look into finding her family." I said.

"What? No, Max. You can't just send her away." she protested.

"Ava, she isn't ours to keep. Maybe she has a father out there that would want his child but we can't just make the decision to keep her." I tried to reason with her.

Right now she is thinking with her heart and not her brain. She saw a neglected child that she can take care of and she doesn't want to let her go.

"Max, I'm asking you to think this through. She deserves better. From what you have said about her mother she must have lived a tough little life." she said as a tear slid down her face.

"I'm telling you no and that's it." I said firmly.

"Well, I want to look into keeping her and we have to make this decision together. You can't just decide on your own." she said as she raised her voice. She was being stubborn and not thinking clearly and I had lost my patience with the whole situation.

"Ava..We are NOT keeping Aurora and that's it. I'm not discussing this shit anymore. Now Justin is working on finding her family and handling the police. I'm going back to the office because this shit is stressful enough without having you fight me on my fucking decisions." I said as I turned around and walked out of the door.

CHAPTER 34

Ava's POV

When the door slammed behind Max I was shocked. I didn't expect him to react so poorly. I understand what he went through but she is an innocent child. She shouldn't have to be put into foster care because her mother is a selfish person.

I calmed down a little bit before walking out to the living room. I needed to relax and think for a minute before I got Aurora from my mother. And I am sure that Noah will be up at any minute now.

When Justin saw me coming he looked up to meet my eyes. I wasn't sure about the look that he gave me. It seemed like an odd mixture of sympathy and disappointment. Usually I would just ignore it but it was something about the odd mixture that wouldn't let me ignore it.

"I'm good at reading facial expressions, Justin. I can understand the sympathy because I am sure that you heard our argument but why the disappointment?" I asked him boldly.

He chuckled dryly before responding. "Because Max needed your support. Even if you felt like what you wanted to do was right he just needed you to back him on this. I get that she is a child but you have no idea what he went through because of that situation."

"Yes I do because he told me." I was a little annoyed at his statement.

"No. He told you what happened. That's different from what he went through, Ava. Max was lost and broken. He was not the man that you have today. He was so hurt and heartbroken that he couldn't do anything for months. He mentally tortured himself over it. I have never seen him so low in my life and I have been his friend since we were four years old, Ava." he said as he looked me into my eyes.

I wasn't sure what to say to that so I just stood there. "I'm not the person to tell you that what you feel is right or wrong. What I am telling you is that Max needed you. I'm sure that mentally he is fucking hurting from this psycho bitch again even though he may not say anything. He would do anything for you and you know that. The fact that he didn't immediately give in to you should tell you something."

I knew that he was right. I should have listened to him or at least spoken to him within reason and heard his side of things. "Thanks,

Justin. You're a great friend to Max."

"Always."

"After I feed Noah I'm going to go talk to him." I wanted to make sure that he knew that I was on his side. That my feelings do not mean that I don't care how he feels.

"Okay, but after the detectives are done at Audrey's they are going to come here to talk with you and Max."

"Did they find anything?"

"Yeah. Audrey is confirmed dead but I don't know anything else." I couldn't stop the gasp from my mouth. Sure she had done some bad things but no one deserved to die.

I grabbed Noah from his crib and walked down to the family room where my mama was sitting with Aurora. While I fed him I had to sit and listen to my mother scold me about not being more understanding with Max. Her last statement stuck with me.

"Pick your battles. When he is in a war you are too but you should be at his side and not against him. Y'all need to talk about this in a better way." she said.

After feeding Noah I set Aurora up with a snack and headed into the office. When I got there I suddenly became nervous. I had never been the cause of Max's anger until today so I didn't know how to handle it but I would do whatever it takes.

When I stepped into his office he looked up from his laptop. "What are you doing here?" he asked.

"I wanted to talk to you." He sighed deeply.

"Ava, I don't want to argue about this." he said in a low voice. I could tell that he was upset.

"I don't want to argue either but I wanted to check on you and I wanted to tell you that I'm sorry for arguing in the first place." I said as I pushed his chair back and stood in front of him and leaned on his desk.

He moved forward and laid his head on my stomach and took a deep breath. I rubbed my hand through his hair and I could feel the tension leaving him. I realize now how stressed he was and how I had made it worse.

"I love you, Max. I hate that you have to go through this. I want you to know that I respect your decisions. I want you to know that I have your back and I will be here for you."

He lifted his head and looked me into my eyes. "But?" he said.

"H-how did you know there was a but?"

"Because I know you. Now what is it?"

"While you all are looking for her family can *I* watch her? I just don't want her to go into the system if we can get her to her family. I promise that you won't have to deal with her. I will make sure that she is settled before you come home. I understand that you hate her being there."

"Fuck, Ava. Don't say it like that. She is an innocent kid. I don't hate the fact that she is there. I hate the situation and I wanted you to understand that she isn't ours to keep. Am I happy that she arrived on my doorstep after what happened when she was born, no. But I could never use the word hate for a child." I was about to respond when his phone rang.

"Yeah…Okay. We will be there in a minute. Watch everything that they do and say to her and tell Ava's mother to take Noah to the family room. I don't want him around any of it." he said before hanging up and looking at me. "Let's go. The police are there and they are about to see if they can get Aurora to tell them what happened."

When we stepped into the house they were finishing up talking to Aurora. She didn't seem too upset but I'm guessing that the story is easier to tell on the second go around. After she was done Max asked me to take her to my mother before we talked to the police.

It took a few minutes to leave her because she clung to me. I felt bad for what she was going through. Her mother didn't think one time about what she would possibly be putting her child through. I know that she didn't because as a mother I couldn't imagine thinking about it and not changing my actions for my child.

When I stepped back into the living room the guys were already talking to the detective. "Max, you know that I'm not supposed to give those kinds of details out when it's an ongoing investigation but I will because it's you." the detective said.

"What's going on? What did I miss?" I asked.

"A lot. Apparently Audrey had journals of all of her crimes. It's all fucking bad. Her scamming days goes all the way back to when she was sixteen. What she did to me was minor." Max said.

"What about the baby?"

"The baby is mentioned in the book but just what she did to Max and also that her mother thinks that Max is the father which explains why she left her at your door. She does not mention who the father is but we are still going through her journals. Maybe we will find something." the detective said.

Max looked at me for a moment before he spoke again. "Jack, we…umm…we need to do some paperwork to temporarily keep Aurora until her father is found. Can you get someone to contact us for that?" I could have just hugged and kissed him right there.

I know that he was doing this for me and I love him so much for it. "Gotcha. I will be in touch." the detective said before leaving. After he was out of the door I hugged Max tight.

"Thank you...Thank you so much." I said and he slightly smiled.

CHAPTER 35

Max's POV

This has been one crazy fucking day. I couldn't have ever imagined that my day would have turned into this. It turns out that my ex and her mother were both bat shit crazy. I'm embarrassed to say that I was ever in love with a person like her.

The things that we have learned about Audrey is fucking mind blowing. For one, her and her mother started scamming a long time ago. Her own mother got her started. She would dress her up and put her on makeup to look older so that she could attract older men.

Once they got close or attempted to sleep with her that's when they would reveal her real age. They would promise to keep quiet in exchange for money but if the guys didn't pay they would threaten to expose them as child molesters.

That was just the beginning. The guy that she was dating in college before me was left before their wedding too but when she left him she didn't leave empty handed. He came from a wealthy family and had loads of cash and valuables that were stolen.

Me. Well, I was supposed to be her long term meal ticket. I was supposed to be the idiot that made them rich until I messed it up by wanting to get married. She had a list of other crimes from credit card fraud to stealing from wealthy people's homes after befriending them.

The crazy part is she was doing a lot of this while I was traveling for work. I feel like a damn fool to have gotten mixed up in this. I had to apologize to Justin because he always said that it was something about her that didn't seem right to him. I made sure that he knew that I was thankful that he had my back through it all.

We were about to wrap this shit up for the rest of the day because I was done dealing with it for the moment. I just wanted to go and lay up with my family. Justin was packing his things up to head home but I'm sure that he is going home and continuing to work on this.

"I was thinking about something earlier and wanted to ask you about it." I said to Justin.

"Yeah. What is it?"

"Remember when Audrey came back and you mentioned that you looked into her. Well, maybe someone that she had been associating with around that time is the father. Maybe ask a few of them discreetly and see what you can find out."

"I will do that but are you okay with this? I mean it can't be easy. I know that you're doing this for Ava but..." he trailed off but I understood what he wanted to say.

"I will be fine. Just don't tell your woman about any of this shit for now. I can see her now trying to bring Audrey back to life so that she can kill her." We both laughed at how crazy my sister is.

After he left I walked down the hall to check on everyone. Noah was already sleeping so I walked down to see where Ava was. I heard her voice coming from the room that Aurora was staying in so I stopped outside the door and peeped in.

They were cuddled in bed together and Ava was reading her book. I was trying to wrap my head around the whole situation but I could see that it would be hard to separate the two of them. I was lost in my own thoughts when I heard someone clear their throat. Since my mother in law was the only other person here I knew it was her.

"Come here, son. Let me talk to you." she said and we walked down the hall a little bit. I was caught off guard when she pulled me into a hug. "How are you feeling?"

"I'm okay."

"No you're not. This can't be easy for you." she said and I shook my head.

"No. It's definitely not easy."

"And my daughter isn't making this any easier." she said and I just laughed a little.

"You take real good care of Ava. You make sure that she has everything that she wants and needs and I don't just mean material things. But, Max, I want you to understand that what she wants does not override what you need. You are allowed to feel the way that you feel and you don't need to feel guilty about any decision that you make, okay." she said and I nodded my head and gave her a small smile.

I honestly needed to hear that because I was thinking about how much Ava wanted to keep Aurora. Seeing the determination in her eyes had me second guessing myself. I'm not trying to be an asshole and of course I wouldn't want to see the baby grow up in foster care. I just want Ava to understand that if we can find her father he has a right to his child. Because knowing Audrey this man has no idea that he even has a child.

I went to my home office for a little while to give Ava time to get Aurora to bed. I wanted to finish up what I had to do as quickly as possible because I was exhausted. Usually I would be up a lot later once Ava and Noah was sleep but today was fucking draining.

Ava came in a little while later. She just stood at the door. "Hey." I said as I looked up. "Is everything okay?" I asked her and nodded her head.

"Yeah. Come to bed with me."

I closed down my computer and we went to our room. We showered and then we crawled into bed and made love. Tonight was different though. I could tell that she was feeling needy and unsure of herself so I poured myself into her slowly.

I can't remember a time when we had sex and it didn't turn heated at some point but not tonight. Tonight I intentionally took my time moving in and out of her and when we finally exploded together it was like nothing we had ever experienced.

When I climbed off of her she snuggled up to my chest and drifted off to sleep. It took me a while to finally start falling asleep but before I could I heard a scream. I rushed out of bed and down to the room that Aurora was in.

She was crying and pulling on the covers like she was trying to hide from something or someone. I ran to her and she started crying harder. "Don't hurt me." she mumbled and it broke my heart. I can't imagine the things that this little girl has seen.

"Aurora, it's me Max. Open your eyes for me, sweetheart." I said as I tried to soften my voice. She slowly opened her eyes and lowered the blanket. When she saw me she opened her arms and reached for me. I picked her up and held her while she cried in my arms. I slowly rubbed her back to calm her.

"It's okay, sweetheart. Nothing and no one can hurt you here. It's okay." I said calmly. After a while she calmed down completely and eventually fell back asleep. When I went to lay her down she clung to me like a little monkey and opened her big eyes as tears formed in them. Oh fuck. What am I going to do now?

Ava would have to be up in a while to feed Noah since he was strictly on her breasts. She didn't even pump so I wasn't going to wake her. I walked down to the family room and sat down on the plush couch and laid back so she could rest.

I turned on the tv and decided to watch a movie while I could hopefully get her to relax. I wasn't sure how long I had been asleep when I felt Ava rub my arm. She was feeding Noah and looking like she was about to start crying...again.

"What's wrong, Angel? Why are you upset?"

"I-I'm sorry. I didn't hear her. I know that I promised that you wouldn't have..." I cut her off because she didn't need to be upset over this.

"Angel, it's fine. Go feed the baby and get some sleep. I'm good." I said as I looked into her eyes. She nodded her head and headed back to the nursery.

Eventually I fell back asleep until waking up to a stirring Aurora around five because she was hungry. I wasn't surprised since she didn't eat much yesterday but Jesus Christ.

I dragged myself out of the family room and down to the kitchen to feed her and of course she wouldn't go back to sleep. A while later Ava came walking into the room slowly with Noah. "Hi." she said softly.

"Hey."

"Umm…I know that you have a lot to do. You go ahead and I will take her." she said softly.

"Okay, Angel." I said before leaning in and kissing her. Her emotions have been all over the place. I will be glad when this shit is over.

CHAPTER 36

Max's POV

As much as I would have liked to head back to bed I needed to get to the office. There was plenty of shit to be done. The main thing was figuring out Aurora's situation so that life can move on. At the moment I am unsure of what I would do if we can't find her father.

I thought about a lot of things and honestly I don't think that I would be able to let her go into foster care, not when I have the means to take care of her and a woman that's willing to. Whatever is going to happen I just want it to be done so our lives can get back to what they are supposed to be.

I don't want to deal with the emotional bullshit that's coming from it and I definitely don't want Ava to. She hasn't been the best emotionally since she had Noah. It's like she always needs reassurance which I don't mind giving but now she is emotional as well because of this and I don't like it.

FIGHTING LOVE

I took a shower, got dressed, and headed to the office. I had gotten a text from Justin a couple of hours ago saying that he had some news for me. I have no doubt that he has probably worked the whole night.

When I walked into the office he was already waiting for me. "Fuck, Justin. How long have you been waiting?" I asked.

"Not long at all. I just wanted to tell you what I found as soon as possible." I nodded my head in understanding but my mind was cloudy as hell.

"So...I possibly found Aurora's father." he said and I was fucking shocked. Shit it hasn't even been a day. "I have been at it all fucking night. I was waking people up left and right. From the information I kept I looked into the groups that Ava was hanging out with at the time. I checked with all of those people to see if there was a common man that she was dealing with and one name came up several times."

"Who?"

"Mark." he said and I had to pause.

"Mark Weathers?" I asked him and he nodded his head.

"Apparently she scammed him too. Well sort of. She tricked him into believing that you were mistreating and controlling her. She pretended to need to get away from you so he was willing to help. So when everything went down he was shocked to find out the truth about y'all splitting up. That's when he knew that she had been lying to him. My sources said that he was pretty pissed about the situation. All I know is that he is the only name that keeps coming up so I sent him a text asking him to meet you around nine this morning."

I didn't really know how to feel about the situation. Me and Mark were friends. At the time we were just associates but we are pretty close now and he never said a word.

"Fuck, Justin. I mean…I really don't know what to say." I said honestly. Do I give a damn about Audrey now? No, but still as a friend he should have told me something.

A few minutes before nine Mark came walking in. "Hey, Max. I was told that you wanted to see me." he said.

"I do." I nodded my head.

"Is something wrong with the company?" he asked nervously.

I invested in Mark's dream company. And they were currently under an audit but it was a normal routine audit. You get the money you need from me and every now and then you get audited. Simple.

"Everything with the company is fine but I

was hoping that you would help me out with something. I have some questions for you."

"Okay. What is it?"

"Audrey." was all I said and he swallowed hard and put his head down.

"Max...I...I don't know what to say."

"Mark, I could give a damn what Audrey did because that's just the type of person that she is. But I thought you were better than that...I thought that we were better than that."

"You're right...Its just...I fucking believed her. At the time we weren't as close and she was very good at lying and manipulating. She made it seem like you were mistreating her and that she didn't want to leave you even though things weren't going well. At first it was just her crying on my shoulder and then one night we slept together." he said before pausing and just looking at me.

"When she left you I had no idea what happened. She made it seem like she had finally gotten the courage to put you behind her. We spent a week together. I never had any intentions on being with her but she said she needed a place to stay at that moment. We did sleep together during that week. One morning I woke up to her gone along with $50,000."

"Wait...$50,000...That's why you were short when you were going to purchase your business?" I asked and he nodded his head.

"Yeah…And I know that it was wrong to come to you after sleeping with Audrey but I was desperate. You know that I worked hard to get away from where I was raised. I saved that money up and it was my only chance to get started." His eyes were pleading with me to understand.

We have known each other since college. I had plenty of money so when he came to me saying that he was short and his deadline was in two days I didn't bat an eye. I have invested even more since then.

"When you found out the truth about what happened, why didn't you come to me?" I asked. "I should have. I know that I should have but I was angry and embarrassed. I didn't want you to take my company from me. I'm sorry, Max."

"Okay." he looked at me confusingly.

"Okay? You're not upset with me?" he asked.

"No. I'm not. I'm over Audrey and her bullshit. Even from death she is still trying to screw me over."

"W-what do you mean death?"

"Audrey is dead. We found out yesterday when her daughter was left on my doorstep. Now the thing that I need your help with…We did a lot of research and it seems that Aurora could possibly be your baby."

"What the fuck?" He got up and started pacing. "What do you mean?"

"We checked around. During that time her sights were only set on me and you. The baby isn't mine. Would you be willing to take a blood test?" I asked him. He nodded his head but he looked terrified for some reason.

"Justin has communicated with the lab. They are going to rush the test. We will have the results in six hours." I said and he just nodded his head.

Mark and Aurora were swabbed and six hours later we were looking at the results. Mark was Aurora's father. "Fuck." he groaned, looking like he was about to pass out.

"What are you going to do, Mark? You don't want her?" I had to ask. I didn't take him for someone that would abandon their child.

"Of course I want my fucking daughter. It's not that...I know that I don't deserve your help but I need you to watch Aurora for another day or two... It's just that I have to talk to Lauren. I never told you this but we have been going through some things. We were trying to have a baby and it wasn't happening so we went to the doctors and found out that she couldn't carry a baby. So yes I want my daughter but I need to talk to her. I don't want to just show up with Aurora."

I nodded my head in agreement because I

understood and knew that this would be hard for them. Audrey once again is screwing someone over. Had she been up front with him this would have gone a different way.

"How was she when you got her?"

"Mark...You don't want to know."

"I want to know. I need to know." he pleaded.

"They delivered her to my old apartment building in a damn box. The doorman thought it was an important package so he delivered the box to my house. When Ava opened it up, Aurora was in there. She was knocked out by something and dirty as hell."

"They put my fucking daughter in a box...Who does shit like that?" he said through gritted teeth.

"I have no idea. They are still investigating everything. Don't let Audrey or the anger destroy your life. Focus on your daughter." I wanted to make sure that he didn't spiral like I did. I let Audrey destroy me at some point but I won't let her do that to him and his family.

"Do you have a picture of her? Can I see her?" he asked. I pulled my phone out and showed him the picture that I took this morning when she was eating.

When he looked at the picture he took a deep breath and I could see his eyes tear up. "She looks just like my mother when she was a little girl." he said with a smile.

"We will look after her, Mark. Go home and talk to Lauren." He left and I left right behind him. I needed to go home and prepare Ava because she was attached from the moment that she opened that box.

When I got home Ava and the babies were sitting in the family room. I don't know what the look was on my face but her face looked concerned when she saw me. She stood up and walked over and so did Aurora.

"Hey, Angel." I said before kissing her and Noah. Aurora lifted her hands to me and I picked her up. "Hello, sweetheart." I said before kissing her on the cheek.

"Max?" Ava said.

"We found him." I said and tears instantly formed in her eyes.

CHAPTER 37

Mark's POV

I'm still finding it hard to breathe after leaving Max's office. I can't believe that I have a daughter. A four year old daughter that I did not know about. My daughter was out here living in God knows what kind of conditions and I had no idea.

When Justin said that Max needed to speak to me this was the last thing that I was expecting but I am happy to have her. I just don't know what to say to my wife.

My wife. My sweet wife that's gentle and perfect in all of her ways. She has been by my side since the day that she came into my life. We got married quickly and tried to start a family for a long time.

Lauren loves children and her desire to be a mother is as strong as our desire for each other. Even though I have plenty of money she still works at the children's hospital just because she loves the children.

So when we found out that she couldn't conceive it was devastating. She cried for days and there was nothing that I could do to take away her pain. Now I have to go to her and tell her that I have a child.

I have to look her in the face and ask her to accept it but the hard part is I want her to be Aurora's mother because she doesn't have one. But I can't just say that to her. And I just don't know what to say or how to ease this on her.

Today just so happens to be her day off so I know that she is home binge watching one of her shows. When I pull up to our house I say a silent prayer that this doesn't hurt her too much because I would hate that.

When I walked in she was laying on the couch watching tv like I suspected. When she saw me she sat up quickly. "Hey. You're home early." she said with a smile on her face. At that moment everything that I had planned to say had gone out of my mind.

"Mark...Honey, what's wrong?" she asked with a worried look. Words failed me. I didn't know what to say. I dropped to my knees in front of her and just laid my head in her lap. What am I supposed to say to her?

"Honey...Please say something. You're scaring me." she said with a slight tremble in her voice.

"I-I'm sorry."

"Why are you sorry? Talk to me." I knew that I needed to just say it. Prolonging it was only going to make her worry.

"Max called me in for a meeting today." I said slowly.

"Okay. Is the company okay?"

"Yes, sweetheart. It was about a personal matter. Do you remember what I told you happened between me and Max's ex?"

I told her the story when we first met because it wasn't long after the Audrey situation. I knew she was the one and I didn't want to hide anything from her. A friend of mine told me that I shouldn't have said anything since it was before her but now I am glad that I did. It makes this a little better to explain.

"Yes. I remember." she said softly.

"Well, he wanted to talk to me because Audrey's daughter was left on his doorstep. After he did some research he found out about me and Audrey and called me in for a meeting. He asked me to take a blood test that he had rushed and it came back six hours later…She's mine. She's my daughter." I said the last part after lifting my head and looking into her eyes.

"What?"

"Her name is Aurora and she is my daughter. She is four years old and I swear that I didn't know but Lauren, I'm all that she has. Her mother is dead."

She had tears streaming down her face and I couldn't stand to see the hurt in her eyes anymore so I put my head down. "I'm sorry." I said again. After what felt like forever she finally spoke.

"Get up." she said.

"Lauren…Please." I said in a panic. "Please listen to me." She squeezed my hand and looked at me.

"Mark, get off of your knees and sit next to me so that we can talk." she said firmly.

I got up and sat next to her. "Now. Tell me what we are dealing with. I want to know it all." I told her everything that Max told me about Audrey from the scamming to my daughter being left in a box.

I don't know if she was more upset about Aurora or more angry at Audrey but her emotions were all over the place. She leaned in my arms and cried. She screamed and yelled and cursed which is not usually her thing.

Then she calmed down completely. She wiped her face and looked me in my eyes. "When do we pick up our daughter?" she asked and I couldn't stop the tears that came into my eyes.

"You-you're going to help me raise her?" I asked.

"Of course. What, did you plan on divorcing me?" she smirked.

"Definitely not but I just didn't know if it would be too hard for you. You know since we can't.." my words died after that. I couldn't bring myself to say it. My head was slightly down because I was trying to reel in my emotions from all of this.

Lauren lifted my head with her hand. "We can't have children and her mother wasn't capable of being a mother. The Lord just used her to give us our child. Now Mr.Weathers, when do we get to see our daughter?"

I couldn't respond. I just hugged her tight and thanked God for her. I don't know what I did to deserve her but I sure am grateful.

"I will call Max in the morning." I said when I was finally able to speak.

"Call him tonight. Tell him that we will be there in the morning."

"Okay but, Lauren, this might not be real easy. She has been through a trauma. We may have to help her through some things." I said, hoping that she wouldn't hesitate. She just smiled and got up and started moving around, grabbing her phone and keys.

"Where are you going?" I asked.

"I'm calling my mom and sister to meet me at the furniture store and Target. I have to prepare the house for Aurora. Can you ask Max what her sizes are and text me?"

"Yeah. Yeah. I will." was all that I could say. God, I love that woman.

When Lauren came back a few hours later with her mom and sister they had way more shit than a little bit. Her mom and sister were surprisingly extremely supportive of it all. They put in a lot of work setting up Aurora's room. Now all that is left to do is bring her home.

When morning came I had barely slept. I was nervous and excited at the same time. I wasn't sure how things would go. When we got to Max's house that morning I thought that I would burst from excitement.

Before we got out of the car Lauren grabbed my hand. "Mark...We didn't talk about this before but I want...I want to be her mother. I want you to tell her that I am her mother." she said and I just broke down in tears again.

I was once again thankful for my wife. Of course I wanted her to be Aurora's mother but I hadn't asked her that. I didn't want to put her through anything emotionally and here she is once again offering herself to not only me but also to my child, our child.

We finally calmed down and walked to the door. Max was already standing there. "Hey." he said and for some reason he looked nervous too.

"Hey, man." I said as I blew out a breath. "It's going to be fine. We sort of prepared her." he said and I nodded.

When we stepped in Ava was walking into the room with Aurora. I had to fight the urge to run to her and grab her. I didn't want to traumatize her any more than she already was though.

"Ava, this is Mark's wife Lauren." Max introduced them because I was too stunned to say anything. "Come here, Aurora." Max said. When she got to him he lifted her up.

"Do you remember when I said that I wasn't your dad but that your dad was a really good friend of mine?" he asked and she said yes. "Well, this is my friend Mark. This is your dad."

I was nervous as shit. Aurora looked at me and she waved. "Hi, Aurora. Can I hug you?" I asked and she came into my arms as if it was normal. I was overcome with joy.

"Who's the pretty lady?" she asked in a small voice.

She was hugging me but her eyes were stuck on Lauren. "This is Lauren. Lauren is my wife and… she is your mother." I choked out. Lauren was rubbing my back to comfort me but she was crying too and so was Ava.

Aurora immediately reached for Lauren. I can't

imagine what she may have gone through. Just hearing that Lauren is her mother had her crying and hugging her tight. "I-I always wanted a mommy." she said between tears.

That broke me to a point that Max had to take me down to his office so I wouldn't lose it in front of Aurora. "Fuck that woman for what she did to my baby. How could she do this to her?" I yelled.

Max stayed silent. He let me get my anger out. He probably is the only person in the world that knows how I feel because the same woman broke him too.

I had to get myself together because I refuse to allow this woman to affect me and my family. The only thing that matters to me right now is Lauren and Aurora. I have my wife and I have my daughter. My life is about to be a whole lot sweeter.

CHAPTER 38

Ava's POV

"Get up. Get up. Get up, Max. Today is the day." I said excitedly as I shook him awake.

"Ugh...Calm down. What time is it?" he asked. "It's almost seven."

"Are you serious? She won't be here until eleven. I'm getting another hour." he said before turning over.

I was too excited to go back to sleep. It's the first time that we will see Aurora since she left almost three weeks ago. The transition went about as smooth as it could have but it did take some patience.

On the day that Mark and Lauren came it was emotional and painful. Mark was extremely angry over the things that Aurora had experienced. Lauren was emotional over it all and Aurora was experiencing a lot of emotions at once.

She was happy to have parents but she was also a little afraid. My mom watched her for a moment so that the adults could talk or more like me and Lauren. Mark was too upset to think rationally and Max just didn't know what to do with the situation.

Me and Lauren decided that it would be best if we didn't immediately move Aurora to their house. She has found comfort and protection in me and Max and we didn't want to further traumatize her by changing that suddenly.

Aurora stayed at our house three more days but she wasn't alone. Lauren refused to leave her. She said that she thought that it was best if she knew that they would be there for her no matter what. When she had a bad dream or needed something Lauren and I handled it together and she was right, it helped Aurora to know that she could trust them.

When the third day came they took her home. We agreed that she needed to be home for a couple of weeks before we could see her again. She needed to get used to the fact that they were her parents and that their home is now hers.

From what Lauren has said it worked. She loves being home. She has met both of her grandmothers and her aunt from Lauren's side and her cousins. She is enjoying being with them already. Now that she is settled they will be coming over to visit for lunch.

I was so excited to see her and her progress. I was already up and getting prepared. By the time that eleven got here I was standing at the door waiting.

"Calm down a bit. You don't want to scare her." Max said. I really did need to calm down. When they arrived she looked so happy. Just as I had predicted she was stuck to Lauren like glue.

"Turns out she is all about her mama." Mark said with a shrug and we all laughed.

I was so happy for them. It's still so crazy how everything happened but it has brought so much joy to them. "So…We kind of wanted to talk with you all about something." Mark said. He was looking nervous which in turn made me nervous.

"Ava, do you mind if I step in the kitchen with Aurora? You stay though." Lauren said.

"Sure. There is some fruit that's sitting out if she wants a snack."

"What is it, Mark?" Max asked impatiently.

"Look…I know that Audrey put you through hell. I know that you also went through a lot when it comes to Aurora so it's difficult to ask you this but Lauren and I just want to be selfish and ask you anyway."

"Just say it, Mark." Max groaned. He is so

impatient sometimes.

"I don't look at Aurora as she is a part of Audrey. She is all mine and all Lauren's. We are thankful to have her and that wouldn't have happened if it wasn't for you. So we wanted to know if you could look past her as Audrey's child and only see her as ours because we want you all to be her Godparents. There is no one else that we would want to be her Godparents but you all."

By the time that he was done I was teary eyed. I wasn't sure how Max felt so I was nervous.Then after a few seconds Max smiled. "Of course we would be happy to be her Godparents. She is all yours, man." he said.

I squealed with excitement causing them both to laugh. "I'm so happy that everything worked out for the best. She is so happy to be with you all." I said

"Yeah she really is. I was scared that it would be a difficult adjustment but it hasn't been. She loves the shit out of Lauren. It's like I don't exist to the two of them sometimes. It's a great feeling to see them both happy." he said with nothing but love in his eyes.

We spent the rest of the evening together having a great time. It was amazing getting to know Lauren. She really did love Aurora as her own. I don't think that this situation could have turned out to be any better than it did, even if we had of kept her ourselves.

Once they left for the evening it was good to just sit back and relax for a while. Now it was just me, Max, and Noah at the house. My mom had finally gone back home after Aurora was settled with Mark and Lauren.

I was extremely thankful for her being here and for her help but I was definitely happy when she went back home. She stayed here way longer than she originally planned but I had a mild case of postpartum after having Noah and I needed her.

Most of the time I was extremely emotional and I always had this fear that I wasn't going to be enough for Max and Noah. He had done his best to reassure me but it was a rough time for me mentally. Thankfully I was starting to get better and now things are going great.

"I'm so glad that we can have some time for ourselves now after all of the drama." Max said.

"Yeah. Me too. It's been a lot." I would help Aurora all over again if I had to but I can't lie. This situation was extremely tough.

"I know and I am so thankful for your patience. I know that it was even harder since it was right after Noah was born but we got through it." he said with a smile before he leaned in and kissed me.

"I love you, Max." I said after our kiss.

"I love you too. Now that we have everyone

else's drama out of the way we can focus on more important matters."

"More important matters like what?"

"Like you being my wife. When do you want to get married?"

"Umm...Anytime you're ready. We can get married tomorrow if you want." I teased him.

"Don't tease me because I can call my mama right now and she will have that wedding together for tomorrow. So, Angel, don't test me because a flight can leave here to get your family in an hour." he smirked.

I sat there opening and closing my mouth because I wasn't sure what to say to him. "Relax. No need to stress. I was only joking, sort of. Now, when would you really like to get married?"

"In three months. I need time to plan so three months seems reasonable for you to wait, Mr.Knight."

"Okay, three months and three months only, Mrs.Knight."

EPILOGUE

Max's POV(a year later)

It's been one hell of a year. After all of the drama died down life fell back into a calmness. We had our little family and we just rolled back into our daily lives as if everything hadn't just been turned upside down for a little while.

We had gotten married exactly three months from the day that we discussed it. We got married on our own property that was transformed into an amazing venue. Ava was very specific and being married at our house was not something that she was willing to compromise on.

Ava's entire family came up and we made it a big deal. We had events leading up to the wedding for a week and then the day came when I finally got to marry my Angel.

She was the most beautiful bride that I had ever seen and she looked every bit of the angel that she is. Aurora, our sweet little Goddaughter, was our little flower girl and loved every minute of it.

She was still doing great at home. We still spend a lot of time with her as her Godparents and honestly it feels great. I'm glad that everything worked the way it did because not only does she deserve loving parents but Mark and Lauren also deserved to be parents to that amazing little girl.

A few weeks after that whole incident the detectives called to notify us that they had found Audrey's mother. She had skipped town and was trying to go into hiding. She knew that her and Audrey had scammed the wrong person and she ran to save herself.

She claimed to have been trying to do her best by Aurora by getting her to me. If you ask me that's all bullshit. You can google me and find out where my office building is. Surely leaving her at my office building would have been better than leaving her in a fucking box.

The only good thing from her doing that is Aurora is safe. She is where she belongs. She now has a loving mother and father. Thankfully Audrey's mother is in jail for her list of crimes and we will never have to worry about her again.

Me and Ava couldn't have been better right now. She is still working in the office to a certain point. She isn't one of the staff members anymore but more like we run the business together. She is included in everything and it's honestly less stressful. We share the burdens and the decisions when it comes to the company.

I get to live peacefully knowing that her and Noah are with me some days and she gets to work with some of the things that she is passionate about. Since we had Noah and Aurora came along she had a new hobby which was all things baby.

She is currently putting together plans to open up some stores that would sell only things for babies and children. The store will sell anything from baby clothes to kids furniture. She loves it so I do as well.

It's funny how life can change over time. A few years back I thought that I was done with all relationships. I never planned on committing to another person but then my shy, well, used to be shy woman came into my life.

I don't know what would have happened had I not lost my shit that night at that party. Cammy still laughs about that today but she is one to talk. All of that damn crying she did when I damn near choked Tyler is unforgettable too. She damn near quit when that happened so I like to remind her of that when she gets to teasing me.

My life has changed from being completely closed off to being sort of opened. I have my family, friends, and even a few new ones. Now the only thing that is left for me to do is knock Ava up again.

A few months after we got married Justin and

Lindsey did too. To be honest I am surprised that they waited that long. I know if it was me and Ava I would have married her the moment that we could have been together.

I still can't believe the bullshit that my grandfather did but I dealt with him properly. Now he wasn't even allowed in his own company that he built, nor was he allowed anywhere near my family. Even my father had cut him off.

I'm not about to waste my time thinking about negativity though. Today is a happy occasion. We are currently at Lindsey's baby shower. She was eight months into her pregnancy and they are having a little girl.

When they got married no one knew that she was pregnant except for her and Ava. When she was at her reception she made the announcement that they were expecting. Justin was shocked and a little bit mad. No one ever hides things from him so he was upset that she didn't immediately tell him. He said that he didn't want to miss a moment of her pregnancy.

"Can you believe this?" Justin asked as he walked up to me.

"Believe what?" I laughed at the stupid grin on his face.

"We're having a baby." he said and I shook my head.

"How could I not believe it? Every day you come into my office damn near singing about it." I groaned.

"Yeah. I'm just happy, man. I didn't think that we would get here. I thought for sure that she would give up on me." he said sadly. Although things were going good I think it still bothers him that he was forced to stay away from her and that he could have lost her too.

"You deserve this happiness. I appreciate you for everything that you had to sacrifice." I said as I hugged him.

"You deserve it too, man. We both do."

COMING SOON

Chasing Love (Justin and Lindsey's story)

Accepting Love (Tyler and Cammy's story)

Fated Love (Mark and Lauren's story)

You Can Find Me On Facebook Under

Author MJ Mango

BOOKS BY THIS AUTHOR

The Billionaire's Student

Nicole has been going through a rough time over the past few years. When life and debt seems to be getting the upper hand she doesn't know what she will do to fix things. One day billionaire Matthew Lewis offers her the opportunity of a lifetime. But will the money be worth dealing with a controlling and dominant billionaire that's used to getting what he wants with no questions asked. Will Nicole be able to open her mind and heart to possibilities?

Unexpected Love

Adam is a private lawyer for his billionaire best friend Matthew Lewis. To switch places from when they were teens, Adam is a little more outgoing than Matt. He has had his fair share of women to play with too. When Matt needs help with his upcoming wedding he meets the bride's best friend Lisa. Lisa is a wild card. She loves to have a good time and doesn't plan on settling down anytime soon. That is until she is helping her best friend's fiance and meets his best friend Adam. Adam's interest in Lisa is far from what he is used to but the only thing is she needs to be tamed. Lisa can be a bit of a challenge but when it comes to Adam and his desires taming Lisa is a task that he is more than happy to complete. After knowing her completely he knows that for him, losing her is not an option.

Healing

Everyone sees Charlotte as the young, successful, and beautiful doctor that she is. She always smiles and loves her patients. But what everyone doesn't know is that Charlotte has a very abusive and traumatizing past and it doesn't matter how long it has been she still suffers from it every day. Life suddenly changes when her two best friends start dating and moving on in life. She realizes that maybe she wants that too but it won't be easy for her.

Theo is a young and hot doctor that works with Charlotte. Everyone sees him as fun and confident but the only thing that he really is, is lonely. When he first laid eyes on Charlotte he knew that she would be his wife one day. He could feel it. It takes some effort but he finally manages to get her to go on a date with him.

Can they find love with obstacles in their way? Two of those obstacles being Charlotte's two male best friends. Can Charlotte heal from her past in order to have a better future?

Made in the USA
Columbia, SC
04 February 2023